Stories by Contemporary Writers from Shanghai

THE CONFESSION OF

Copyright © 2015 Shanghai Press and Publishing Development Company

This book is edited and designed by the Editorial Committee of *Cultural China* series

Text by Sun Wei
Translation by Yawtsong Lee
Cover Image by Getty Images
Interior Design by Xue Wenqing
Cover Design by Wang Wei

Copy Editor: Susan Luu Xiang
Editor: Wu Yuezhou
Editorial Director: Zhang Yicong

Senior Consultants: Sun Yong, Wu Ying, Yang Xinci
Managing Director and Publisher: Wang Youbu

ISBN: 978-1-60220-251-1

Address any comments about *The Confession of a Bear* to:

Better Link Press
99 Park Ave
New York, NY 10016
USA

or

Shanghai Press and Publishing Development Company
F 7 Donghu Road, Shanghai, China (200031)
Email: comments_betterlinkpress@hotmail.com

Printed in China by Shanghai Donnelley Printing Co., Ltd.

1 3 5 7 9 10 8 6 4 2

THE CONFESSION OF
a Bear

By Sun Wei

Better Link Press

Foreword

This collection of books for English readers consists of short stories and novellas published by writers based in Shanghai. Apart from a few who are immigrants to Shanghai, most of them were born in the city, from the latter part of the 1940s to the 1980s. Some of them had their works published in the late 1970s and the early 1980s; some gained recognition only in the 21st century. The older among them were the focus of the "To the Mountains and Villages" campaign in their youth, and as a result, lived and worked in the villages. The difficult paths of their lives had given them unique experiences and perspectives prior to their eventual return to Shanghai. They took up creative writing for different reasons but all share a creative urge and a love for writing. By profession, some of them are college professors, some literary editors, some directors of literary institutions, some freelance writers and some professional writers. From the individual styles of the authors and the art of their writings, readers can easily detect traces of the authors' own experiences in life, their interests, as well as their aesthetic values. Most of the works in this collection are still written in the realistic style that represents, in a painstakingly fashioned fictional world, the changes of the times in urban and rural life. Having grown up in a more open era, the younger writers have been spared the hardships experienced by their predecessors, and therefore seek greater freedom in their writing. Whatever category of writers they belong to, all of them have gained their rightful places in Chinese literary circles over the last forty years. Shanghai writers tend to favor urban narratives more than other genres of writing. Most of the works in this collection can be characterized as urban literature with Shanghai characteristics, but there are also exceptions.

Called the "Paris of the East," Shanghai was already an international metropolis in the 1920s and 30s. Being the center of China's economy, culture and literature at the time, it housed a majority of writers of importance in the history of modern Chinese literature. The list includes Lu Xun, Guo Moruo, Mao Dun and Ba Jin, who had all written and published prolifically in Shanghai. Now, with Shanghai re-emerging as a globalized metropolis, the Shanghai writers who have appeared on the literary scene in the last forty years all face new challenges and literary quests of the times. I am confident that some of the older writers will produce new masterpieces. As for the fledging new generation of writers, we naturally expect them to go far in their long writing careers ahead of them. In due course, we will also introduce those writers who did not make it into this collection.

Wang Jiren
Series Editor

I

Legend has it that the Shucun villagers originally lived on the other side of the Himalayas. Due to tribal rivalries their forefathers were forced to abandon their homes in order to flee the carnage and their flight took them all the way to the Hengduan Mountains. For forty-nine days they marched, and they still had not put towering peaks, a landscape strewn with forbidding boulders, and dark forests behind them. Birds and beasts often stopped to gawk at these refugees, as if they had never seen humans before. Now the flatbread and the dried meat on which they had subsisted were depleted, and wild berries and vegetables could not stave off the pangs of hunger. Their clothes were torn and their shoes were worn down in the long march. The lineage was threatened by imminent extinction before they reached safe haven.

Zhewa the Elder mounted the tallest rock he could find, gashed his palm with his sword, took the long bow made of silkworm thorn from his shoulder, drew a falcon feather-tipped arrow from his quiver and released it into the air with his bleeding hand, praying that the gods would lead them out of the jungle to a land of sanctuary.

With a whiz, the arrow disappeared in a blue sky finely fragmented by the leaves and branches of the forest. Zhewa the Elder, guided by the call of the arrow which only he seemed to hear, led his people onward. Everyone became swift of foot again, a new urgency and expectation in their tread.

The towering trees that had hemmed them in began to recede and all of a sudden their eyes were dazzled by a sunlit panorama.

They saw foothills with low vegetation that descended into five small plains in five different directions, much like a fully open flower with five petals growing in the midst of uninhabited forests, mountain peaks, and gorges. It faced south and was sheltered from the wind. There, larks sang in the woods, squirrels skittered from branch to branch, and fawns walked unconcernedly by. Not far down from their feet the Jinsha River roared by, throwing up snow-white foamy crests.

In the meantime, that arrow guided by the gods was standing quietly near a clear brook, planted in the soil of a plot of land that needed no further clearing or leveling for dwellings to be erected on it straightaway. On the other side of the brook lay swaths of wild wheat already golden and ripe for harvesting. This was indeed a home given by the gods! In confused awe and elation, they prostrated themselves to give thanks to the gods for the blessing.

As their foreheads touched the warm soil, the quiet earth beneath their knees suddenly started trembling and a fantastic roar reached their ears from all sides. They could not tell if it was the sound of the shaking of the leaves and branches of massive trees in the wind, or the crashing of the waves of the Jinsha River on its banks, or a peal of thunder in a perfectly clear day. As they wondered, shadows converged from all directions and eclipsed the sunlight on the green grass. They looked up, half rising from the ground, and all strength drained from their legs. They saw bears; not one, but hundreds, maybe thousands of them, emerging from tree roots, low mounds, among tufts of grass and flowering shrubs, much as mushrooms growing under big trees on a rainy day. These plump, stocky figures standing erect not far from the tribesmen eyed them in silence.

The average height of these bears was comparable to that of humans of shorter stature, but they possessed two or three times the mass of an average man. They had round ears, shiny black fur and a white patch at their neck shaped like a crescent moon with its horns pointing upwards. What is most striking to the observer was an almost human face between the black tufts of hair at the temples, a milky white chin, a flat mouth, and small eyes. These upright bears standing in neat formations gave the impression of grotesque-looking, corpulent local villagers dressed in black hooded jackets gathered to challenge the interlopers with sabers drawn and ready to defend their home.

Escape was hardly possible. More bears were springing up out of the ground and now numbered more than the trees in the surrounding forests. Even the habitually calm and composed Zhewa the Elder could not stop the muscles in his face from twitching and quivering, for he knew only too well that a bear standing upright was a bear poised for attack, and the force of a swinging bear's paw would instantly break the bones of even a strong bullock, not to mention a man. Zhewa closed his eyes in despair, waiting for his final moment.

As his fate hung by a thread, a flash of light cleaved the sky, brighter and stronger than sunlight. In that light he felt a sensation of warmth enveloping his body. Am I already dead and on my way to the netherworld? He wondered. Fortunately he was not feeling any pain, by the mercy of his gods! Out of curiosity he opened his eyes a crack to have a peek at the road that his soul had embarked upon. In his partially obstructed view a cloud radiating a brilliant golden glow was moving toward where they were prostrated, its dazzle bringing tears to his eyes. At its approach the nine hundred ninety-nine species of fauna and flora dispersed and the bears with a human face densely carpeting the hillsides parted to make a wide path for the moving light.

The moment the blinding light went out, Zhewa saw before him a humongous bear, its height reaching straight into the clouds and its whole body luminescent. It had a splendid reddish brown coat, a powerful head, and the strong build of a bullock. When it walked slowly on all fours, it appeared at a distance to be a moving mountain, with a massive, bulging, muscular back, and bulky shoulders. "This must be the Bull Bear of legend, the god of bears!" Zhewa cried with wonder to himself.

In the awed silence, the Bull Bear walked at a slow, regal pace, his pelt glistening in the sun. His every footfall was so light it gave an impression of not wanting to hurt the grass underfoot. With a calm composure and half-closed eyes warm and mellow like water, he walked in the manner of a king touring his realm. As his eyes swept past the beings lying at his feet, they felt calm and warmth hitherto unknown to them and, strangely, no fear at all. He paused and turned his head around to take a sweeping survey of the bears with a human face gathered in formations. Where his eyes, like a wind sweeping through the woods, landed, the bears let fall their front paws and dropped them to the ground.

With a slight nod at Zhewa the Elder, the Bull Bear turned into a streak of light and disappeared in the hills. Almost at the same moment the land resonated with another earth-shaking roar as the hundreds of bears with a human face turned in a body and disappeared to their caves without a trace. Only sunlight and the shadows of the clouds traveled silently across the smooth grassy plain.

The prostrate humans, as if wakened out of a dream, had a moment of dazed wonderment before regaining the presence of mind to bring their brows back down into contact with the soil to complete their thanksgiving to the gods.

Thus began the settlement of the Shucun villagers on this plain, where they've lived and bred until this day at the border of Yunnan and Sichuan, boasting 272 households in five large tracts of densely spaced dwellings. Shucun village is in the jurisdiction of Xuyang County of Yunnan Province and is unreachable by car, boat, or plane. This virtual isolation from the rest of the world has meant that these people are self-sufficient in food and clothing. They rely on the Elder to preside over weddings and funerals as well as seed sowings. They revere the God of the Bears, worship the Bull Bear as God incarnate and treat the bears with a human face as benefactors and friendly neighbors that have taken them in.

They have observed to this day the prohibition issued by Zhewa the Elder against harming any bear.

Liu Yushan, Deputy County Chief of Xuyang, tall and plump in his middle years, had his hair heavily pomaded and possessed a face bronzed and creased by long exposure to the sun, and eyes that became bloodshot the moment he imbibed alcohol. He was also a chain smoker of Double Happiness cigarettes and when he spun a tale he smoked with a vengeance. He shook his head unapprovingly, with the words "silly and ignorant" quivering on the tip of his tongue, but for some reason decided to hold them back.

"Was there ever another sighting of the Bull Bear?" I asked.

"There was a report by village people putting out ears of corn on their roofs to dry under the sun that they had seen a golden glow in the forest, which they had at first suspected to be a forest fire but the glow was gone in a flash," Liu Yushan answered. "That prompted some to bruit about the manifestation of the God of the Bears. There followed much beating of drums, blowing of trumpets and the killing of sheep and hogs that were offered to the gods. Some woke up to find, when they went to work in the fields, one or two giant foot prints showing five toes, with no follow-on prints that led in any direction. They couldn't have belonged to an ordinary animal, unless it had flown in, landed at the spot and flown out. The morning dew that had accumulated in the depressions, unaccountably, formed contours and outlines strikingly similar to those of the plains of Shucun."

Those were stories that vied in grotesqueness as they were relayed from mouth to mouth and were not to be taken seriously.

"Xiao Liu, are you properly fed?" Liu Yushan asked abruptly as he lights another cigarette. "It's a long way to Shucun village. I think you should leave as early as possible."

I happen to share the same family name as Liu Yushan. Like him, I am also rotund of body, although much fairer and finer in complexion. Nonetheless, one plump face and another often looked quite alike. For that reason the deputy county chief warmed to me immediately and right away refer to me as *xiao ben jia*, a term of endearment that was something like "my young cousin." Then he went further and everyone he could get hold of, he asked rhetorically if we look like father and son. And throwing his heavy arm around my shoulders, he shoved and paraded me around until I felt almost light headed.

The fact is there was no way that this deputy county chief and I could be perceived as father and son. I realized that he was only forty-six and I was over thirty-four. It was only due to the different environments in which we had lived that he looked much older than his age and I had kept my youthful look. I didn't feel comfortable being called "Xiao Liu" either. In my company, indeed, in almost all foreign or pseudo-foreign companies in Shanghai, people call each other by their English names. My English name is Kevin, which I have used in more than a decade of hopping from one Global 500 company to another.

Fourteen months ago, I was once again at the privileged forefront of the layoff list of my company. The downsizing was attributed to the economic crisis. It seemed I never had any luck with foreign companies. It took me two or three years to be promoted to a supervisory position, but in seven or eight years, after those I had once supervised were given managerial jobs, I stayed a mere supervisor. Every time there is a campaign of sending cadres into the field, salary cuts or layoffs, I never fail to figure prominently on the list of candidates.

This time around, after a hiatus of twelve months of unemployment, I got hired by HZ Communications China. But before my chair in the prime commercial real estate in downtown Shanghai was warmed by my behind, I was again sent into the field. Dressed in Calvin Klein attire, carrying an Emporio Armani attaché case and a Montblanc pen in my shirt pocket, I flew all the way from Pudong Airport in Shanghai to Kunming, where my company has an office. From there I traveled by car and, after days of driving, arrived at long last in this little town at the border of Sichuan Province, hemmed in by tall peaks crowned by dense clouds.

Come to think of it, were it not for the misplaced paternal affection of Liu Yushan, I would not have been able to make so much progress in so short a time in my work. I had arrived only yesterday morning by the overnight long-distance bus. Mr. Liu, the deputy county chief, had dinner with me and this morning he came during breakfast to grace me with his presence, and the best car in the county government motor pool was placed at my service and was now parked outside. This was my transportation to the Shucun village.

This best car, allegedly once a Mazda SUV, looked as though it were only a few years my junior and after many successive replacements of parts, traces of its former self were almost all gone. As I depressed the pedal to drive up the road leading into the mountains, I could still see Liu Yushan in the rear view mirror waving to me from a distance. Ahead of me was an inky sky threatening rain, and a chain of mountains whose ridge resembled the ripple-like furry back of a divine beast, ornamented by splashes of spring blooms and veiled in mists.

I revved the engine up the ascending road and as the car made a turn around a bend, Liu Yushan and the county town of black-tiled single-level houses vanished behind me. The puny car was swallowed in the folds of the mountain spurs, surrounded by the soughing of winds blowing through the giant trees.

II

HZ Communications China was founded four years ago by the parent company HZ, headquartered in the Asia-Pacific region, with the ambition of becoming the largest equipment manufacturer in its specialized field in China.

In its eagerness to win the contract of supplying networking communications equipment and services to China Mobile for its markets in Jiangxi, Yunnan, Sichuan, and Fujian provinces, and in order to build and foster, in advance of the contract tender, a glittering, positive public image for itself, HZ Communications China offered, in collaboration with Yunnan Mobile, a gift of a satellite phone to the remote and impoverished Shucun village. And I was the sole company representative sent on a field trip to Shucun as part of this public relations campaign.

I'd been on the road for a good four hours and it was one o'clock in the afternoon. After eating one and a half steamed buns I still had a whole bag of them left. Two canisters of gasoline went into the tank of the car and four remained, sitting in the back seat. According to the detailed map Deputy County Chief Liu gave me this morning, at the end of the motor road I was to leave the car and walk on for another four hours until I came to a plain in the shape of five petals with five large aggregations of houses with shale-tiled roofs. That would be the Shucun village. He had hoped I would postpone my trip by a day so that he could accompany me tomorrow. He couldn't get away today because he had meetings to attend. The idea of spending a day more than I had to in this place in the middle of nowhere did not appeal to me. "All right, you can't miss it," he said. "There's only one trail leading to the village."

The mountain road was recognizable as such only intermittently. It was not infrequent for the tires to scrape the lush leaves of ferns, throwing up fragments of foliage and twigs that gave off an intense herbal fragrance. The foreshadowed rain did not materialize as clouds and mists dissipated. Thin shafts of sunlight peeked out from distant clouds, much like a stingy spotlight seeking out the chosen people of God lost in this vast wilderness.

I stepped on the gas to head into that patch of sunlight when suddenly something like a ball of fire, or perhaps a lightning bolt rolling down the side of the mountain, blocked my way. It was a brilliance that defied description—golden red, like the softest core of a flame. It spread like afterglow in a sunset and was accompanied by an earth-shattering rumble. Leaves started raining down from the trees in the dense forest and vegetation and rocks dimmed, as if the entire world, under the shock of this brilliance, had absconded into negative film. Even the image imprinted on my retina turned in half a second into a transient negative image.

I instinctively tried to stop the car by stepping on the brake pedal, but the car was going a bit too fast and the brakes were a little worse for wear and the car kept hurtling until it crashed with a racket into something like a soft wall. The light instantly went out, like spent fireworks. I was knocked out of my wind as I hit the steering wheel, hurting my ribs in the process. My forehead crashed into the windshield. The crazy-quilt world through the cracked glass rolled ninety degrees to the left and I, cramped and stuck in the car seat, fell to the right toward the ground. An even louder racket of things tearing and splitting apart followed. Then total darkness and a blank.

I remembered wrapping my hands in my sleeves to protect them against the broken glass when I clambered out of the twisted car door.

The car looked like a crumpled cardboard box.

To the left of the front end of the car lay a huge beast with reddish brown fur. The size of three all-terrain vehicles combined, it sprawled in the middle of the road like a hill with a fantastic color, its chest heaving in uneven breathing; after a few jerks, it did not succeed in its attempt to stand up. In all likelihood, it had rushed down the side of the hill next to the road and came right into the path of the car and was hit in the chest and abdomen, the softest parts of its torso.

When I staggered past the humongous beast, my knees suddenly started quaking. Less than a hundred meters ahead, that beautiful sheaf of light filtering down through the clouds was trained serenely on the mists rising from the bottom of a precipice. The deceptively wide and level mountain road came to an abrupt end here, without any forewarning, dropping off into an abyss. I saw nothing under my feet but puffs of clouds and vapors hugging the sheer cliff.

If my car had continued to travel another hundred meters, I would have gone over the cliff. Most probably I would at this moment still be airborne in a free fall, shrieking in terror and describing a parabolic arc through space like a grotesque, sheet metal bird.

With a tumultuous churning in my chest I lost consciousness.

III

My body was in a constant swinging motion.

I had no sensation in my hands and feet and I couldn't move.

My back bumped against rocks and my shoulders hurt as if they were dislocated.

I forced my swollen eyes open and saw the blue sky oscillate right and left about an axis constituted by a wooden pole. My hands and feet were tethered to the pole and my body slung on the pole was carried by two men. The glare of the sun prevented me from having a clear view of their faces except for strings of some dainty little moon-white ornaments dangling from their long plaits that tinkled with each step they took. They appeared to be tiny animal teeth of various kinds.

During one stage of the march, my body hung over a chasm. With every swaying motion, I could glimpse out of the corner of my eyes the lush abyss. I was terror-stricken, fearing that I could be let go and tumble into that deep, bottomless maw. I had an urge to scream but I was slung over a pole with hands and feet tied together, and my broken ribs hurt so much I couldn't produce a sound.

I could vaguely discern, at the foot of the deep gorge, the contours of a green flower with five petals, crowned by glistening cyan pistils. The veins on the petals seemed to outline a neat patchwork of planting fields. A weathered voice was singing *hu-*

ma-hu-ma-la-ni-yeh, hu-ma-hu-ma-ge-la-jia. Strangely the voice, while by no means orotund, sounded as if it had traveled a great distance, feeble but articulate, breathing every word into my ears. Peace and serenity entered the sense of hearing and radiated out into infinite space, and my pale, plump soul once again floated out of the body.

IV

Truth be told, I got my present job at HZ Communications China through the help of my one-time girlfriend Jessica. She very tactfully expressed her disappointment with me. I was working at HZ then, headquartered in the Asia-Pacific region. She had a job with MG at the time. In my successive hops from company to company, I never managed to catch up with her as she moved up the corporate ladder.

Following my layoff, the stock market plummeted to 1,000 and new entries on help wanted websites almost dried up. I sent out my CV to dozens of places without getting a job offer. After being out of work for six months, I shed my pride and started asking old colleagues for help. Michael, Manager of Human Resources at the HZ Asia-Pacific headquarters, told me there was nothing he could do for me, but a subsidiary newly set up by HZ was expanding its operations and might need people.

"Kevin, don't you know?" he added with a sly laugh over the phone. "That Jessica of yours has joined HZ Communications from MG. She is now the sales manager there and enjoys great popularity and respect. I understand that the two of you have kept up with each other all these years. With her in that position, there's no reason she can't find a suitable job for you. By the way, she has not had a boyfriend since breaking up with you. She is the legendary Iceberg Beauty of HZ."

As a last resort and with the greatest reluctance, I went to see Jessica. It was our first meeting since she moved out of our apartment. We sat on the balcony of the Starbucks inside the Metro City Mall in Xujiahui District on an off day in autumn, enjoying the last sunshine of the year, drinking cappuccino and eating blueberry pie. She was the typical Shanghai girl with delicate, regular features—eyebrows painted into two slim arcs, an oval face, large eyes with lashes that fluttered non-stop like the wings of a butterfly, and the inevitable paper napkin in her left hand that constantly went up to dab at her mouth (a stack of napkins would thus be killed off before a cup of hot frothed beverage was finished).

She looked even more beautiful than six years before. Her hair was shorter now, falling down to her shoulders and slightly curled, framing a face with smooth, well-fleshed out cheeks. A glittering platinum Guanyin pendant dangled on her necklace. Her French manicured nails discreetly showed off the smooth, white complexion of the fingers wrapped around the coffee cup. Her eyes no longer shifted and wandered, but often held mine with a smile. This added to her attractiveness but often forced me to avert my eyes in blushing embarrassment.

"Why don't we do this," she said in a soft, even tone. "You come to the sales department and help me out. I will talk to human resources."

A job, that's what I'd been aspiring to! But I really hated to put Jessica out.

"It's very easy," she said, as if guessing my thoughts. "The job opening has been there for quite some time now and hasn't been filled for lack of suitable candidates. Human resources would thank me for it."

On Tuesday I was notified to go to the personnel department to fill out a staff registration form. I was familiar with this procedure at HZ. It would be followed by the formalities of recruitment. I hadn't expected it to go so smoothly. When Jessica accompanied me to the personnel department to pick up the form, we met Carl in the corridor. For the shortest moment Carl had a startled look but he recovered quickly and came over with a big smile to give me a few pats on the shoulder. I caught a fleeting look of embarrassment as he did so.

Carl and I went back a long time. During the two years I worked as an employee at the Asia-Pacific headquarters of HZ and the four years I was chief of procurement, I watched as he rose through the ranks from a salesman to sales manager. At the annual meeting of the company held at the Sheraton Resort Hotel on the beachfront of Yalong Bay in Sanya in Hainan Province, the two of us basked in our success. I was rated the star of cost control for that year and he, in an exhibition of the full panoply of his excellent qualities as a sales expert, gave the only speech that did not induce sleep at the convention.

He was tall, liked to play tennis, and had at the time the physique of an athlete. He was always dressed in a smart suit and wore a neat crew cut. His oblong face with a shiny forehead was never without its warm, friendly signature smile. His faultless Mandarin and English with a British accent, spoken with great variations in tone and inflection, conveyed an enthusiasm that proved contagious and gave an impression that he was an orator whenever he opened his mouth. We had had no interaction at the workplace and had only heard about each other. That convention finally brought the two mutual admirers face to face. At the formal dinner we drank a lot of Merlot together and afterwards in the lobby bar commanding a view of the beach we finished half a bottle of Chivas Regal between us as we talked about women.

Now Carl had gained some girth at the waist but had otherwise changed little. Only he was now a vice president of HZ Communications. "So it's Jessica who got you to apply at our company?" Carl said. "I didn't know that. Excellent! Now we'll be working together again! Welcome!"

With that he solemnly offered to shake my hand in a very formal gesture of welcome, as if this was already my first day at work. The grip of his hand instantly reassured me and I privately congratulated myself. After filling out the forms, I was seen to the elevator by Jessica and suddenly realized I was humming a tune. Fortunately, Jessica didn't seem to have heard it and as she said goodbye she appeared somehow to be absent-minded and anxious to leave.

A week went by, and then a month. I went down every day to check my mailbox and went online three times to scan through my emails, but still no notification of hiring decisions or reporting to work. Strangely and uncharacteristically, Jessica had of late been offline all the time on MSN. My pride prevented me from calling her on the phone to make any inquiries. I could only tell myself, wait, and wait some more.

Six weeks later, no longer able to stand the anxiety that was eating me up inside, I finally decided to call Jessica. She seemed to be occupied with something and only acknowledged having heard me with perfunctory hems and haws and was noncommittal. I swallowed my pride by repeating my questions.

"Why don't you send an email to Carl and ask him?" she said. "Didn't he promise you a job last time you met? His responsibilities now include overseeing personnel matters in consultation with human resources."

Ten minutes later I received an email from Jessica, the kind of formal, work-related email so familiar to me in the past. It read, in English: "Dear Kevin, how are you? This is Carl's office email, please contact him directly. Best regards." It was followed by Jessica's electronic signature in Chinese and English.

I was puzzled. Didn't Jessica say it was very easy and that the company was eager to fill the vacancy but had not been able to find a suitable candidate? I had thought the matter would be clinched with the agreement of Jessica and human resources. Why did I have to go through Carl also?

I couldn't very well demand an explanation from Jessica. When she said she'd help me find a job, I had struck a lukewarm pose. How could I now give an impression of total dependence on her? There was no alternative but to follow her suggestion.

After much consideration and a dozen revisions, I finally fired off an email stripped of all emotion to Carl, asking him if his "distinguished company" had arrived at an opinion either for or against hiring me after reviewing the application form I filled out.

Before business closing time the following day I received Carl's response, in which he disclosed that the matter was still under examination and consideration and had not been submitted to him by the personnel department and expressed deep regret about the long wait the applicant was subjected to. It was a short, correct but hollow letter that had probably been drafted by his secretary. But I saw a ray of hope toward the end of the message, for Carl added: "Hey, pal, don't forget your old friend. Come in and have a chat when you pass by someday." The body of the text was written in formal English, here at the end he sounded familiar.

Working up enough courage I decided to "pass by," thinking this was in all likelihood the only opportunity to produce movement in the matter. On a sunny morning I rode the subway to the Huangpi Road station and took the exit for the Pacific Mall on Huaihai Road. I killed time by strolling through the streets and then came to the lower level of the Hong Kong Grand Century Place Mall and stood idly for a while before dialing Carl's office number, making sure he would hear the noise of the shopping crowd. "I happen to 'pass by' your office building, how about my bringing up a coffee for you?" I was going to say casually and cheerfully to him.

The moment I said a hearty hello, I found it was his secretary who took the call. She asked in a businesslike manner for my name, position, and reason for the call and told me to hold. Minutes later she informed me that Carl agreed to see me after 2:00 PM.

Before going to the appointment with Carl, I "passed by" Jessica's office. I did this as an emotional warm-up to the manufactured chance meeting with Carl and also to reconnoiter for signs of the possible hitch in my job application. Jessica's first reaction when she saw me wave at her from the door was one of astonishment, followed by delighted surprise. She put down the file in her hands and came to the door to let me in. She invited me to sit with her for a while in her office and had her secretary bring me a cup of coffee.

When she learned I was here to see Carl, her delight seemed all the greater. "You did the right thing," she said. "It's high time that you get together and have a good chat. After all, you're no strangers to each other. You were always so naïve about such things."

To my very casual question about the matter of my job application, she replied by asking me if I was on a diet because she found me thinner than before. Without waiting for an answer, she said abruptly, "Carl is my superior. You've done the right thing by coming to see him on your own." Then she bade me goodbye, saying she had business to attend to.

In ignorance and confusion I rode up in the elevator and walked the length of the corridor to the door of Carl's office. His secretary checked my name and the time of appointment on her agenda book before admitting me. Carl didn't put on airs, although his enormous desk and the high-backed leather chair were somewhat intimidating. For about half an hour we talked about the weather, soccer, and old gossip going back to our days at HZ Asia-Pacific headquarters. Then I finally summoned the courage to broach the matter of my job application.

"I really miss the nine-to-five days," I started to say. "Sitting idly at home with nothing to occupy me is tough."

He took a quick glance at his watch and assumed a startled look. "Oh, I nearly forgot I have a meeting at two thirty. Time really flies when old friends chat. It was a real pleasure, Kevin. Do come again when you have the time."

With that he rose to his feet and offered his hand. It was a warm, forceful handshake. He left me with no alternative but to make for the door, albeit hesitatingly. At the door I turned my head around and said embarrassedly: "My job application …"

He appeared to have anticipated the question. Looking up from the dossier he was reading, he nodded with a smile. "We'll talk about it some other time."

The secretary in the meantime had opened the door and was waiting on her feet for me to leave. After I came out of the inner office of the vice president, the secretary opened the door to the corridor.

V

*X*ia-lu-wa, xia-lu-wa, xia-lu-wa!

The rhythmic sound assailed my ears from all sides, as if I were surrounded by a huge crowd chanting in unison. This constant assault on my eardrums wakened my soul.

Where was I? The deafening sound caused ringing in my ears and a splitting headache.

Through the narrow cracks between the eyelids I forced open with great effort, I gradually made out a very large room in darkness, with no lights, except for slivers of sunlight filtered through cracks in the brick walls casting a smattering of points of light on the sooty walls and floor. Further away in the middle of the room a shaft of light came down at an angle, its outline substantiated by the rising smoke and floating dust in the room. A puny figure, whose hands were busy doing something, crouched by the fire pit under a skylight.

It had the feel of a scene from a dream.

I found myself propped on a pile of firewood in a corner of the room, my back chafing against the prickling twigs. I tried to shift the position of my body, only to find that I was still bound by ropes. My hands and feet were now free, but my torso was securely wound in coils of hemp ropes. When I tried to take a deep breath, a sharp pain in my ribcage elicited an involuntary scream from me. The echoes of the scream startled me. So I was not dreaming after all!

At the sound of my pained cry, the ambient shouting, as if on cue, went decibels higher. *Xia-lu-wa, xia-lu-wa!* The points of light on the walls shifted and shimmered. There was really a noisy, impatient crowd gathered outside obviously.

In a panic I started shouting uncontrollably, "Untie me! Untie me! Where am I? Who are you?"

In response, the shouting of the crowd became even louder. *Xia-lu-wa, xia-lu-wa, xia-lu-wa!*

Then I saw the puny figure crouching by the fire pit stand up and walk with a light tread and at a deliberate pace to the door, push it open and say something in a soft tone. The shouting ebbed, and there followed the sound of receding feet scattering in different directions, and the points of light on the walls were restored one after another and became steady again.

But the sound out of me did not abate; I could hear my own scream for a long time. It was prompted by an uncontrollable terror. Finally, drenched in sweat, I fell silent. I had shouted myself hoarse.

In the enforced quiet I suddenly became aware of a third living being in the room besides me and that puny figure. Two eyes the size of tennis balls squinted half closed were spying on me, about three meters from me near the wall, eyes with a naïve twinkle mixed with interest and curiosity.

Seeing that I had finally sensed its presence, the being winked one of its eyes and suddenly moved its furry face to rest its chin on the floor, and, opening wide its mouth, it gave a huge yawn. Its mouth was as wide as the span of a palm, and opened to reveal two rows of sharp, white teeth. What I had thought to be an amorphous pile of earth occupying a space of about four square meters next to one wall, I realized now, was in fact the inert form of this being that had hitherto been lying quietly. When it yawned, its back heaved and the reddish brown fur on its impressive bulk gave off a wondrous luster in the dim light.

I recognized it now. This was the enormous beast that was injured when it came into the path of my car.

A man and a beast were put up in the same half of the room. But our treatments couldn't be more different. I was thrown onto a stack of firewood while that beast lay comfortably on a thick mat of hemp. I was bound up while it was free to move about and had before it four or five wooden bowls containing honey, dried fish, smoked meat, golden kernels of wheat, and bright red nandina berries. A king's feast, if you will.

Then I was suddenly reminded of the story told by Liu Yushan. Could this beast be the Bull Bear of legend, the God of the Shucun villagers?

What a disaster! Why did I pick their God to crash into right on their turf? I reckoned that the most likely scenario was that the Shucun villagers found the two of us lying on the ground and transported us back to their village. They would naturally do their best to restore health to their God. As for me, someone who had the temerity to hurt their God, my prospects were dire. Would I be served up to the Bull Bear, just like the dried fish, the smoked meat, and the rest?

In great fright, I put my feet down on the floor and moved sharply back, and losing my balance, fell off the stack of firewood and landed with a racket on the floor. But the puny figure remained seated by the fire pit, seemingly oblivious to the great noise, the deft movements of the hands continuing without the slightest pause or hesitation.

In the shaft of light sent down from the skylight sat two wooden barrels, from one of which the puny figure took some powdery stuff and mixed it with a dark red liquid ladled out from the other barrel. Soon, in the manner of a dove flying out of the hand of a magician, a dark red fawn materialized with all its limbs. On the floor illuminated by the shaft of light stood already three longs columns of horses, deer, cows, sheep, and other animals I couldn't name. The work continued without letup. The dust picked out by the shaft of light danced about the seamed, soft and serene face.

"Granny!" I cried with all my might. "Granny, help me!" All I managed to get out was a hissing sound trapped in my throat and tears rolling down my cheeks. I was ignored.

VI

In the two weeks since I "passed by" Carl's office I waited anxiously but heard nothing back. I considered "passing by" his office in the Hong Kong Grand Century Place a second time, but remembering the awkwardness of that first episode, I hesitated. Every morning I would wake up about seven o'clock and plan to leave at nine, but would then put it off on various pretexts and surf the Web on my computer until eleven.

I was driving myself mad by this procrastination. By the end of another week of futile waiting, my cell phone rang one morning at ten-thirty. The area code was from the Huaihai Road vicinity and my heart raced. It did indeed come from HZ Communications, and from none other than Carl himself.

At the other end of the line, Carl's laugh sounded cheerful as spring. "Hey, Kevin, I'm so sorry to bother you," he said. "Are you free tomorrow and day after tomorrow? I wonder if you'd be able to help me out. I have two friends visiting from Hong Kong and they will be here in Shanghai this weekend, but unfortunately I'm leaving tonight on a business trip to Beijing. Can you play host to them on my behalf and take them around Shanghai?"

"No problem," I said, only too eager to oblige. "It's only proper that I should do it."

Proper my ass! I kicked myself afterwards for being so

masochistic and self-degrading. After all, the friendship between Carl and me did not go beyond sharing a few drinks one night in the distant past. If he had come to Shanghai from out of town, I wouldn't necessarily have cared to play host to him, let alone entertain his friends on his behalf. And yet I was so obliging, as if he had granted me a favor and a once-in-a-blue-moon opportunity that I didn't even have the presence of mind to ask who would pay the expenses.

Those two visitors from Hong Kong were very demanding, and treated me like some underling designated by Carl to pander to their every need. On Saturday, they clamored to be taken on a tour of the Oriental Pearl Tower, with me, naturally, picking up the tab. In the evening I wined and dined them at a teppanyaki place on Riverside Boulevard and got a paid receipt from the restaurant. Early on Sunday morning I accompanied them to City God Temple, where we had *xiao long bao* dumplings (soup dumplings) the Temple is famous for before I was able finally to hustle them into a cab that took them to the airport. Then I called Carl to report that the two-day excursion was a success.

I could hear the hum typical of a crowded restaurant in the background as he thanked me in a loud voice. "Kevin, you are a good pal! I can accomplish anything with your help!"

That took out of my mouth the question I most wanted to ask. And what he said also essentially shut me up about whom to take the paid receipts to for reimbursement. I allowed Carl to hang up on a got-to-go, cheerful note, comforting myself with the idea that since Carl now owed me a favor, he would actively intercede on my behalf and secure the job for me.

I waited another month without hearing anything from HZ Communications. I began to despair of it. I got ready to scour the help wanted sites online, lower my sights and cast a wide net when sending out my CV. But it was poorly timed, for Christmas was approaching and it was the slowest season of the year for recruitment. Even when a post was advertised, the contact person's heart was not in it. So I temporarily suspended my job search and slept in every day until the sun was high in the morning.

I was wakened out of my sweet dream by the loud musical ringtone of my cell phone. "Kevin, are you free today?" Carl said jovially. "How about playing a round of golf with me?"

I agreed with alacrity. Opening my eyes, I found that day had not broken yet and a pale moon still hung in the sky. Trembling with winter cold, I paid dozens of yuan for a taxi to take me to the golf course on Longdong Boulevard in Pudong. The sun stole across the sky as the cab negotiated the long, bumpy road to the green. I told myself this time I must get a definitive answer about my job. Eighteen holes would be enough time for me to get a clear and detailed answer out of him.

And I got to ask the question. Carl gave me the answer. "HZ is a Global 500 company that countless would-be candidates try to get in. It is public knowledge that HZ Communications China is spearheading HZ's planned expansion in the China region. As a result we get more job applications than we have time to review. They are all talented people. Besides, the company is not really short-handed. The hiring campaigns are only for public consumption, a sort of PR, contrary to what Jessica told you."

"But," Carl continued, "I will try my best to secure a job for you. Have some patience."

In his new position, Carl has acquired new hobbies and tastes. Tennis is a white-collar sport and golf is for the gold collars. He strode with confidence and self-assurance and his swings were graceful and well-practiced, as if he was born for high management. I, on the other hand, struggled and stumbled along, tormented by the freezing suburban temperature, and managed several times to hit the ball into the river. And when I tried to strike a ball by the river, I accidentally landed my foot in the water. It was a wonder that they were able to maintain the green in such unusual lushness even in this weather.

At the end of this day of misery for me, Carl paid for both of us and took me home in his car. This greatly improved my mood.

Without a doubt what perked me up most was his promise to "secure" a job for me. I came down with a serious cold, but there was peace in my mind. It was with deep gratitude to Carl in my heart that I spent New Year's Day with a sniveling runny nose.

Twice in a month I called Carl to say "Happy New Year." On the second occasion, after I'd exhausted all the pleasantries, I hemmed and hawed, loath to hang up.

"It's very difficult," Carl then answered my unspoken question. "The company has suspended its recruitment campaign. But don't you worry! I will do my best on your behalf. Just wait patiently for a while longer."

When February came around, with the Chinese New Year barely a week away, I called Carl again to wish him an early Happy Chinese New Year. "I am busy," he said and hung up impatiently.

Meanwhile, Jessica evaporated from the earth two thirds of the time, leaving MSN messages unanswered and answering my text messages two or three days late and taking my calls one out of three times only. In the six years after we broke up, she had remained in touch on online chats and had always been ready not only to analyze the difficulties I encountered in life, but also to help me untie emotional knots. What had happened to change all that?

On the fourth day of the lunar New Year, I braved ridicule by calling Carl, who was in a surprisingly friendly mood. "Come by my place, will you?" he said.

I thought to myself: "You are inviting me to formally wish you a happy New Year!" So I spent hard-earned money to get two bottles of Château Margaux red and a box of Montecristo cigars and headed straight to Carl's apartment. Carl readily accepted the New Year's gifts and treated me to two cups of fresh brewed coffee and one eighth of a cheese cake and offered me a return gift of two bottles of Chateau Latour. It appeared he didn't try to take advantage of me and had invited me over truly to have a friendly get-together on this festive occasion.

I felt contrite for having misread his generosity of spirit. When there was still no news about the job after the Spring Festival, I decided not to be an awkward burden to Carl and Jessica any longer. I figured that companies would soon start a new round of recruitments and I was all set to start my own job search online when the mailman came with the announcement that a registered letter was waiting for me to pick up with proper ID.

The job offer arrived finally.

The staff registration form I filled out bore the number of 89. When I reported to the personnel department in great elation, I found to my puzzlement and surprise that the others who were there also to complete the formalities of recruitment had the numbers 106, 107, and 108. That meant that during the agonizing five months of waiting for the job offer after I filled out the registration form, seventeen people who filed after me had been hired by the company ahead of me.

On a later occasion when I had coffee with Jessica alone, I mentioned this fact. She averted her eyes and fiddled with the platinum Guanyin pendant on her necklace. Not to embarrass her, I was going to steer away from the topic when she suddenly said something that threw me into confusion.

"Kevin, it's not that I didn't want to have anything to do with you," she said. "It was for your own good. In that situation, I found it inappropriate for me to intercede for you. Some people enjoy feeling important. If things were too easy, their psychological needs would be left unfulfilled."

Carl and I met again when he received me in his office. This time we met not as old colleagues and not for idle chat. Now we worked for the same company again, where he was management and I was on the bottom rung of the corporate ladder. I offered a million thanks and he strode out from behind his enormous desk and patted me on the shoulder, without the least air of superiority, saying I must prove with my sterling performance that he was well justified to give strong backing to my hiring. Then he announced to me that at present there were two departments willing to take me. One was the sales department overseen by Jessica and the other was the marketing department managed by William. He wanted to know which one I'd pick but didn't need an immediate answer. He gave me two days to consider my decision.

"There's no need for further consideration," I said. "I'll go with the marketing department."

On the first day of work at the marketing department, William organized a welcome dinner for me, with the attendance of all the marketing department staff. When Mary timidly said that her nanny had to go home in the evening, leaving her son unattended if she attended the dinner, William waved his hand. "It's your choice," he said. "Do you want to pick Kevin or your son?" And that triggered a ripple of naughty laughter in the office.

William sported a pair of horn-rimmed glasses, had neat, white teeth, and long hair that fell down to his shoulders. He was witty and was the only person in the company to have the air of an artist. Word had it that everyone in the marketing department was his fan. His fan club included even young girls and middle-aged ladies from other departments of the company, who frequently came to the marketing department on the pretext of some kind of official business, or occasionally sat in on a party of the marketing department, for the sole purpose of catching a witticism or two from William.

The welcome dinner was held at Xianghuqing, a restaurant specializing in Hunan cuisine, on a side street two traffic lights away from the company. It boasted an impressive façade but service was slow and sloppy. Buckets and mops sat around, waiting to be removed from the main eating hall, and the private banquet rooms had water stains on their walls and the chairs smelled faintly of mold. I couldn't understand why William preferred this restaurant with no ambiance to speak of, except possibly for the fact that its owner, who was on good terms with William, allowed him to bring his own alcohol. A case of six bottles of Arhus Absolut Vodka of the raspberry flavor, William's favorite, had been carried into the reserved banquet room by Thomas and placed on the tea table.

William had a rule for his parties: There must be alcohol in everyone's glass. For those who couldn't hold their drink, there was the alternative of beer. Out of gratitude for such a generous welcome, I heroically poured myself a full glass of vodka. The proper way to drink this kind of liquor was to do it fast—tilt and empty. Before the hot dishes were served, Thomas had already made me down three glasses of the strong stuff. My job title had been decided before the welcome dinner and I was named PR chief—not too shabby by half. Thomas was my only subordinate in the PR team, a young man with red lips and white cheeks, fresh out of college, delicate like a girl and small in build but self-confident and unafraid to look you in the eye. A favorite expression of his was "I have an old head on young shoulders." His staff registration form bore the number of 90 and he was recruited by the company five months ahead of me, but ended up being a staff member of greater seniority dancing attendance on me.

"Boss, I look forward to a fruitful career under your able leadership," Thomas said in apparent earnest to my face. We drank three glasses to that and soon other colleagues gathered around us, as if by previous agreement. As the hot dishes and the sizzling iron griddle tappan were served, the ambient noise sounded like thousands of water droplets dancing in a wok with boiling oil: a cacophony of conventional toasts, backhanded compliments, slights disguised as intimacy, and gossip and anecdotes bandied about, some familiar and some esoteric to me. Suddenly I felt safe and relaxed, and the tight muscles in my shoulders loosened with an audible click. The cobwebs that had clogged my mind in the recent past were swept away. I finally belonged again, to a collective that had opened its arms to me. I no longer needed to feel haunted by the sense of being deprived of a group identity.

To every toast I responded by throwing back my head and

emptying my glass, feeling toasty and warm in my heart, although the alcohol in my stomach felt cold like fragments of glass. Smiling faces hovered around me. I wanted to have something to eat. I reached for the bean curd strips with my chopsticks and picked up a bunch of them, but they fell off, leaving only two or three strands between the tips of my chopsticks. Mary was propelled toward me. Someone filled a glass with beer and pressed it into her hand. Under her flimsy, single eyelids, there was a look of timid embarrassment.

"Drink it up! Drink it up!" Someone said before she was able to utter a word. She opened her mouth, revealing two disproportionally large front teeth that glinted in the light. "Drink it up! Drink it up!" She choked and covered her mouth, while the tidal waves of voices pressed her to finish the remaining half glass. "Drink it up! Drink it up!" And I threw back my head one more time, or was it two more times? By the time I put down my glass, she had already returned to her seat, and was looking at me with an expression of contrition.

The roast fish was served on a large sizzling griddle warmed by a gas burner. Amid cheers, William rose to his feet and thrust his wine glass in front of mine. "Do you still remember my name?"

"William," I answered with effort. He swept the room with his eyes before shooting me a complicit smile. "No, no, no! What kind of pal are you? How can you forget my name? What punishment do you think you deserve?"

I remember drinking up three consecutive glasses by way of punishment and I flicked my wrist to invert the glass to show not a drop remained in it. "Only casual acquaintances call me William," William said, holding his wine glass in his hand. "You should call me Will. Pals always call me Will. Hey, you really can hold your drink."

I thought I detected some surprise in his eyes. I steadied myself with effort, put a hand to my shirt front, and tried not to knock over my wine glass as I set it down carefully on the table.

"You made another mistake." William's words, indistinct at times, continued to pour into my ears. "You have drunk a toast to everyone around the table except to Will. Come, we must drink this up!"

"All right, let's drink it up!" My voice seemed far away to me. Someone thrust a nice-looking, semi-transparent wine bottle our way and seemed to be filling my glass. A cool liquid washed over my fingernails. I could see William was still holding his glass high. Then a proud smile sprang into his face, much like the expression on the face of a matador bowing to the audience after having pulled out the sword that gave the coup de grace to the bull. My hands dropped to my sides involuntarily. I had a sense that someone was trying to steady my corpulent body. Both my consciousness and my body went into a freefall.

That was indeed a totally enjoyable party and I was happy and touched. That's what I told myself when I woke up the morning after. But my olfactory perception said otherwise. A smell of roast fish permeated my suit and every layer of clothing, down to my underwear, a surfeit of spices infiltrated every fiber. And a strange chemical aftertaste lingered in my gastro-intestinal tract. Raspberry my foot! What kind of additive did they mix into that heady spirit?

I walked into the office with an embarrassed, sheepish air early next morning. A front desk girl who was at the welcome dinner was already standing next to my cubicle, her hands on the back of my swivel chair and a white, bare knee half resting on the seat, twisting her body left and right, tittering as she chatted with William next to her. When she caught sight of me, the hilarity of her tittering, with a hand over her mouth, heightened. "You did really good last night," she said to me.

William came over and gave my shoulder a couple of playful jabs. "From now on, you call me Will."

From that day on I was called on to attend one dinner party after another organized by William almost every other day. At the second one, it was I who took the others out for a drink at the suggestion of William. At each round of dinner parties, people in the marketing department sat down to wine and dine William, all apparently on special terms with him, or more correctly, all in the belief that their group was the only one enjoying favor with Will. Some parties were organized by William for media friends, still others for company brass. The parties came in all sizes, from five or six to a dozen, the only constant being alcohol and inebriation. And unless higher standards were called for, William normally asked his assistant to make those dinner reservations at Xianghuqing Restaurant.

The smells of roast fish and raspberry dogged me. I often stared vacantly in the morning at the work in hand and at the lunchbox at lunch time. When I received an invitation to a party, I'd feel infinitely weary, but when no invitation came, I'd feel unaccountably disappointed. A dinner party can be a quick way to effectively exorcise the anxiety of someone with too much time on his hands and at a loss to know what to do with it and someone dreading aloneness. A dinner party, on its wobbly feet, carries the onerous responsibility of dispensing a sense of belonging, trust and cordiality, and emboldens its participants with alcohol. Yes, I must admit that I get a sense of belonging in those cozy private banquet rooms packed with fellow humans and flowing with food and drink and drowned in noise. But in that briefest moment preceding the plunge into the drunken state, I felt as if I were sitting on the brink of a sheer cliff paved with thousands of smiling faces, impaled by an acute sense of emptiness.

I became a hot item in the marketing department, I was now William's favorite. This was already public knowledge. My worth and stature steadily rose with the increasing number of dinner parties I attended. Everyone showed deference to me in manners and in tone, even though I had not been given any assignment yet, and was still in a phase of "studying" dossiers and cases. Thomas hovered about me all the time, trying to get me to talk, even when there was nothing to talk about, and endeavoring to find common language between us, undaunted by the generation gap.

"Oh, you mean Johnny (Jiang Yuheng) the pop singer? How could I not listen to his songs," he said in an excited, loud voice, as if he had just found a kindred spirit. Backing up a few steps, he pretended to arrange the papers on the desk and gave a few light taps on the keyboard before coming before me again. "Oh, I absolutely adore his *Looking Back a Second Time* and *Quitting You Is Like Quitting Smoking*! I just knew we would have a lot in common and get along. I am more mature than my age would indicate."

He danced about me for the obvious purpose of getting me to take him to the dinner parties. "I am your only subordinate," he said. "We are the same. We should share weal and woe and be always seen together."

He hit the right chord with me and I felt a rush of warmth surge through my body. "Boss, taking an errand boy with you to these parties will be a measure of your importance in the public eye," he added.

At the table Thomas's eyes lit up. He was all worked up and engaged everybody, especially William. When William raised his glass, he would try to beat everybody to be the first to raise his and to say something appropriate for the occasion. At least it saved me a lot of energy and spared me many obligatory shots of liquor. The downside is when there is such a gung ho person at the table the dinner will inevitably drag on for quite some time. Weak-willed as I was, I never had the courage to leave early and always stuck to the bitter end.

Shortly after I began taking Thomas to one of those dinner parties, my invitations to them started to dwindle.

At the end of the work day, Thomas would act mysterious and make a point of telling me he had to leave first. When I went downstairs, I would see him waiting at the elevator, with his back turned toward me and feigning not to have seen me.

He no longer bothered to seek out topics of common interest to us. When I tried to start a chat, he would answer perfunctorily in monosyllables, with his eyes glued to the computer screen and his fingers dancing on the keyboard, apparently too busy for idle chat. Therefore, when Thomas re-exhibited his previous eagerness to talk to me one day, I obviously said too much.

"Boss, why did you pick the marketing department when you had a choice between marketing and sales?" Thomas asked.

"It was because of Jessica," I said. I told him in broad strokes that there had been a special relationship between Jessica and me and that in order to avoid the embarrassment of working in uncomfortably close proximity, I had decided against going into sales.

That greatly piqued the interest of Thomas, who avidly probed into the nature of my special relationship with the Iceberg Beauty of the company. Lured on by the natural pleasure in two men talking about a beautiful woman and driven by that damnable vanity of mine, I revealed that Jessica had been my former girlfriend. In retrospect, that indiscreet conversation probably paved the way for my exile to faraway Shucun village.

At a regularly scheduled Monday meeting, a discussion was initiated about how to implement the company's ambitious bidding plan. With any eye to burnishing his credentials, Carl was committed to winning China Mobile's telecom network equipment contracts for six provinces, reportedly worth 800 million yuan. Jessica was made head of the bidding team. The marketing department was to launch a PR campaign in support of the bidding effort. One of the highlights of the campaign was the donation of a set of satellite phone equipment to the impoverished, remote mountainous areas of Yunnan Province with a view to boosting HZ Communications' image of good corporate citizenship.

"Let's go American for once and hold a democratic election," William said in an apparent good mood, before adjusting his eyeglasses with a broad smile. "Let's see which team will be picked to go out to the field on this idyllic trip."

For a few hushed minutes, people exchanged glances and

looked away unconcernedly. William acted like a cheerful game show host, reeling off one name after another of the team leaders. A few hands were raised then lowered. Finally he pronounced the name of Kevin. Before I realized my name was called, a forest of hands sprang up before my eyes. Nearly everyone voted for me. As they kept their hands in the air, some looked out the window and others stared at me pokerfaced.

VII

A grayish black pig, its four hooves tied together, was slung on a pole and carried by two men to the raised platform. The posture of the pig reminded me of the way I was carried into Shucun village.

The sky was overcast all the way to the horizon. The clouds, like layers of ink strokes, hung low. The surrounding mountains, whose outlines were fudged by the fogs, became one with the sky. In the clearing, hundreds of people, men, women, old and young, had gathered, all dressed in cross-front upper garments of hand-woven cloth and baggy pants; their plaited tresses were ornamented with pendants consisting of bone-colored animal teeth and tusks. They formed a large amorphous, haphazard circle around the platform raised on a dozen harvested ginkgo tree trunks of equal size.

When the pig slung on the pole was brought closer to the platform, an agitation rippled through the milling crowd. The sight of the pig drew their feet forward and the circle closed in. Only the kids, oblivious to what went on about them, were still weaving between the adults' legs, absorbed in their own games involving mud and stones.

That puny figure I had seen creating clay animal figurines in the middle of that big house was now draped in a long gown with embroidered hems and edgings and wore a tall, six-peaked hat with gold inlays. He stood at the left of the platform, facing the crowd, with his wrinkled left hand raised. A few days before, I had found out that he was not an old granny, but an elderly man with facial features uncharacteristically soft for a man. He was the current Elder of Shucun village. His name was Shuren.

Lifting his left hand and touching the tip of his middle finger to his forehead, he kept his eyes closed and remained silent for a while. Pastel colors of red and white were applied to his forehead and there was blue paint on his cheek prominences. Then without warning he stretched out his hand with the palm facing skyward and snapped open his eyes, at which moment screams erupted from all directions. *Xia-lu-wa, xia-lu-wa, xia-lu-wa!* A crescendo of voices gradually fell in with one common rhythm.

Two men immediately laid low the pig and another two came forward to hold it down securely, forcing one side of its face into the ground, leaving a beady, rolling, puzzled eye in the other side straining to look up at the sky. There was a sudden pitiable wail accompanied by a desperate thrashing of its four hooves upon the earth. A sharp knife was unsheathed, raised high, and with a glint arcing through the air, was plunged once, twice, and thrice into the creature. A frenzied cheer went up from the crowd, drowning out the increasingly shrill, painful howling of the pig. Even the children had stopped their games and had insinuated themselves to the front row to gawk. Reflected in their dark, glowing pupils was blood that kept spreading until it soaked through the large tract of sandy ground on which the four strong men were standing.

I must have peed in my pants because I felt a warm wetness in the seat of my pants. I was positioned at the other side of the platform, securely bound up with ropes, left there like another head of cattle. I knew they were gathered to invoke blessings upon their Bull Bear. Obviously, in their logic, lives had to be taken as a sacrifice to ward off evil so that the Bull Bear would recover from its injuries.

Two more stout men detached themselves from the crowd and lifted me up, one on each side of me, and threw me down, landing me right beside the pig. Another round of loud cheering erupted from the crowd. *Xia-lu-wa, xia-lu-wa!* Squirming and wriggling, I tried to say something in my defence but knew it would be all to no avail. No one here understood the language of Han Chinese, something I had been unprepared for when I set out for Shucun. Nor did they speak Tibetan, much less English. The way they pronounced their vernacular sounded closer to ancient Sanskrit. It was a linguistic system generally foreign to me, but I correctly guessed the meaning of this chant. *Xia-lu-wa* meant "kill him." My ears had been inundated by the sound of this chant hundreds of times already in the past few days.

I half rose on my knees, in a last-ditch attempt to struggle free. At that moment Shuren pressed down on my shoulders. "*Chee-ma-lah-lee-aye-jia-duh, ma-coo-joo-loo-tah-mi-kah-lah-aye-jia-duh.*" This was not addressed to me but to the crowd that was surging forth. After uttering those words, he suddenly bent down and translated them for me in awkward Han Chinese. He was telling them humans are too impure, far more so than animals and therefore are unfit for being sacrificed to the gods.

His voice was soft and low, no louder than a whisper, but was extremely clear amid the thunderous clamors of hundreds of people. The excitement of the crowd gradually subsided. But I could still feel the slight tremors of the ground. The four hooves of the pig were still thrashing, until the twitching finally stopped.

For the first time in days I was unbound.

The crowd had dispersed. On the raised platform sat the severed head of the pig, its tail and hooves, as well as the hundred or so dark red miniature animal figurines, which Shuren had spent days making by mixing pig's blood with glutinous rice paste. The color of those pillars supporting the platform was quite suspect. I had thought at first they were turned brown by long exposure to rain and wind, but now I could see blood slowly seeping into the wood grain.

Two kids were laughing boisterously at the foot of the platform, fighting each other to stab with a twig at something resembling a small ball. It appeared to be a fun toy, bouncing about and unbreakable even after being stabbed multiple times. It turned out to be the heart of a pig, which had retained its elasticity and was still blood-smeared.

I was well aware that I was still a prisoner awaiting execution on an indeterminate date. Shuren told me that the villagers had agreed to allow me to live among them for the moment, until the recovery of the Bull Bear. I knew that Shuren spoke Han Chinese poorly, but he had made an effort in choosing his wording, just to make me feel better. The truth behind those words should be if the Bull Bear was on the way to recovery, I would be returned to my world. On the other hand, if it should die from its injuries, then I would not escape the retribution of a life for a life. For now though, I could relax during a kind of reprieve. After all, even a pig being readied for sacrifice had to be fed properly.

Light was failing. I tiptoed around the edge of the platform and seeing no one around I surreptitiously quickened my steps toward a low hill. I passed through a large pasture between two clusters of village houses and started racing toward the forest. A sprinkling of people was moving about in front of some village houses at a distance, others were working the fields on a hill further away. I was sure no one had noticed me, and even if they had, I would be too far away for them to catch up with me. I finally came to the edge of the woods. I believed that once I entered this vast dark palace, they no longer would be able to find me among these gigantic, densely intertwined tree trunks and branches, in this impenetrable space lurking with unsuspected dangers. Suddenly, there was a shriek, apparently the sound of some strange bird calling in the depth of the wood. I backed away a few steps in fright.

From the other side, where the setting sun painted the plain a rosy tint, rose indistinctly the sounds of "*jia-luo-ni-jia-yeh, mo-lo-mo-lo*." People who had been moving about, or bent over the field they were working, everybody, no matter where they found themselves to be, instantly stopped whatever they were doing and turned to stare after the setting sun while repeating in unison after the leading voice. *Jia-luo-ni-jia-yeh, mo-lo-mo-lo.*

The massive shadow of the forest crawled inch by inch closer to cover my body and block the sunlight above me. On the spur of the moment I made a weak-kneed but, I believed, wise decision. I started racing back toward the village. I told myself that before the Bull Bear breathed its last breath, I should still have plenty of time to plan my escape. I could first find out where the road out of the village lay.

By the time I approached, panting, the familiar big house, night had fallen. A candle seemed to be expressly placed on the window sill, lighting the road, as if expecting the return of the chastened would-be escapee.

VIII

Thomas was to have accompanied me on the trip. There was no getting out of it for him and the plane tickets had been purchased with that in mind.

"Kevin, you'll be traveling to a remote part of China," William said to me the day before departure. "Who knows when you'll be able to return? And don't you think you need someone from your team to man the fort here?"

Thomas, who had been taking his time, plenty of time, packing his laptop, returned the laptop to the desk and headed straight to the fountain to make himself a cup of coffee. He appeared to have prior knowledge of the arrangement, for he hadn't shown the least signs of getting ready for travel. I remember he came to work that day carrying his usual shoulder bag, but no suitcase. In the end I went to the airport alone, and the company car that was supposed to take me there was canceled at short notice on account of some other use.

It was so transparent. William and Thomas were complicit in it. I further suspected that Thomas was a spy working for William. My sudden ostracism and exile could only be attributed to Thomas's report to William that Jessica, manager of the sales department, was my former girlfriend, and maybe there was more than meets the eye in our relationship.

When I started working at the marketing department,

Jessica had called to congratulate me. She sounded to be in a magnanimous mood, and didn't even ask why I hadn't chosen her department. I was made to feel somewhat guilty by her magnanimity. A week after her call, on a busy morning, we finally came face to face in an elevator. In anticipation of the warm weather, which was still in the offing, she had changed into an ice blue spring suit, a windbreaker, a silk scarf and a skirt that showed off her white jade-colored calves. She looked perky and attractive.

It was the opportunity I'd been waiting for and I grabbed it. "What a surprise meeting you here! Are you free at lunch time? Why don't we go eat at Zen Restaurant?"

The dinner invitation was long overdue, but, unable to swallow my pride, I kept putting it off.

The elevator was so crowded that once I had turned to speak to her I could no longer turn back around and my eyes had nowhere to rest but directly on her face, at close range. A familiar fragrance wafted from her hair into my nostrils. She was wearing Christian Dior J'adore. She lifted her eyelids to throw me a reproachful glance and briefly curled a corner of her mouth in a smile before quickly extinguishing it.

"All right," she said. "It so happens I have something to talk to you about." It was terse and said in a low voice. As the door opened, I was pushed out of the elevator by the exiting crowd.

She was already seated at a table with upholstered seats by a window when I arrived. She raised a hand to attract my attention. There had to be more than a hundred patrons in the main hall of the restaurant. A girl in a white long skirt was continuously playing the piano. Not knowing what to say, I kept urging her to choose from the menu. She demurely deferred to me by pushing the menu back to me, so I plunged into a perusal of the menu. I thought to myself that she should know what this was about and I shouldn't need to clumsily cast about for the right words to say to her. I was thankful that when the cold hors d'oeuvre was served she flicked her hair back behind her ears and looked at me seriously. That was the characteristic gesture that used to signal she had something important to say to me.

"Kevin," she said, "will you be willing to help me with something?" I nodded with alacrity. I had been fretting about how to return her favor and she just gave me the answer.

"Good, I'm glad," she said with a smile. "You'll not be able to wriggle out of this promise. Word has it that you are now the favorite in the marketing department. Can you keep an eye on William for me? I'd like to find out if there's any chink in the armor of William or the marketing department. I need to have a definite answer as soon as possible. Kevin, with your easy access to William, this shouldn't be difficult, right?"

My chopsticks froze, either in my own bowl or a dish in the middle of the table. I couldn't tell because I was dumbfounded. I came out of my bewilderment to find Jessica still gazing at me, her beautiful fingers twirling the platinum Guanyin pendant on her necklace and her teeth lightly biting her lip.

During that period William took me to dinner parties nearly every day. They invariably ended in us getting stone drunk and hitting each other's shoulder with a playful fist as he insisted on my calling him Will. Jessica was well aware of my closeness to William. Worse, while the blockbuster Hong Kong movie *Infernal Affairs* looked romantic on the screen, in real life what they did in that story could scarcely be called honorable. On the one hand I had no wish to be an unsympathetic person begrudging a favor to a friend, but on the other hand I didn't want to be a dishonorable man, although I had long been judged by Jessica to be a useless man.

"I know William's personality has a way of causing offence," I said haltingly. "He is careless and abusive with words. He likes to show off. Don't pay too much attention to all that. Besides, the marketing department works to support your sales department. Taking him down would not necessarily benefit your department."

Jessica had expected the difficulty of persuading me. "That was uncalled for," she said. "Do you think this is about some personal gripe between me and him? You still don't understand, do you? I am asking you to do this not only for my own sake but also for Carl, and for the future of the company, including your own future."

"As a matter of fact, it is Carl, not me, who wants you to do this," she added. "He personally saw to your recruitment with a view to turning you into someone who can accomplish things for him. He put you in the marketing department so that you could help him identify William's failings that he could use to bring him down."

Did Carl put me in the marketing department? I had thought it was my own choice. Then it suddenly dawned on me that Carl had known how I would choose when he gave me the two choices! I was truly naïve and was so easy to manipulate! I started to feel a tinge of resentment.

Jessica knew me only too well. When she saw the slight shadow on my brow, she already guessed which way the balance in my heart had tipped. She abruptly beat a retreat from the subject. "Let's eat first," she said, laying her hands on the table.

The following day, Carl called me when the office closed for the day. The familiar voice boomed heartily in the phone. "Kevin, you haven't left, have you? Come by my office."

"Yes," I replied with eagerness, "yes!" It was then that William was walking out of his office, carrying his bag in his hand and his windbreaker on his forearm. He jerked a thumb toward the street and I remembered only then that there was another dinner party that night. William was signaling me to leave. "Oh, I don't think I can make it to your office today," I said haltingly into the phone. "I have an engagement tonight."

When Carl spoke again after a silent second, he sounded a little upset. "Kevin, I'm waiting here for you. You come up first before you leave for your engagement."

"Yes," I said promptly again, "yes!" I was puzzled by my reaction. Why was I always reflexively deferential to Carl, heeding his every beck and call? Kevin, drop in when you pass by the

Hong Kong Grand Century Place one of these days. Kevin, play host to my Hong Kong friends for me and take them sightseeing for a couple of days in Shanghai. Kevin, how about a round of golf with me. Then I understood all of a sudden the meaning of the five-month delay in receiving my recruitment notification. It was a game of taming an animal, to condition me to associate his mere voice with good news and gospel, and an edict intimately bound up with the fondest wish of mine. And it worked.

Carl's talk with me was rushed, for I had to tell him that William was waiting downstairs for me to go to the dinner party. If I showed up too late, it would surely trigger his suspicion.

Carl cordially patted me on the shoulder and casually flicked off a fallen hair there. He confirmed to me that the job Jessica wanted to entrust to me was indeed not planned by her but was his idea. He hoped that I would, for the great future of the company, decide to join their camp. Correcting himself, he declared I had been one of them all along, because of our association with each other when we both worked at the Asia-Pacific headquarters, and because it was he who took care of my recruitment into HZ Communications, and also because of Jessica. "Do you really have the heart to let her down?" he asked.

He had to trot out all those reasons naturally because of my continued failure to take a position one way or the other. I would see an anxiously waiting William five minutes after I left here, and would once again drink with him until we both got drunk as a skunk today, ditto tomorrow, likewise the day after. I could hardly imagine how I'd face him if I agreed here to become an accomplice to his downfall.

Carl didn't see me out, but the moment before I walked out of his office, I could hear him say to my back in his British accented English with its pleasant inflections, "Kevin, I know you. You will do it, I'm sure of it. We look forward to hearing from you." He never for a moment faltered in that self-confident tone.

I remember it was a dinner party in the high standards

category. William took me in his Land Rover to the Thai Village Shark Fin Restaurant inside the Grand Soluxe Hotel in the Hongqiao District instead of to the usual Xianghuqing Restaurant.

On the way I puzzled about the possible reason for Carl and Jessica to gang up in a plot for his downfall. What did he do that had so antagonized them? They talked about the future of the company. Could William have been plotting something to the detriment of the interests of the company? I fretted, until I walked into a private banquet room filled with gastronomic delights and radiating a subdued elegance.

Around the table were placed bright red gladioli. Outside the full-length window by the honor seat a stream flowed quietly in the shade of banana plants. The menu had been put together ahead of time and featured braised shark's fin, South African abalone, braised green crab with Vermicelli en Casserole, braised goose feet in abalone sauce, plus Cabernet Sauvignon. My spirit was lifted at the prospect of this sumptuous feast, and the question that had been troubling me was temporarily put out mind, even though I knew all this luxury was not intended for me.

William's honored guest was the president of HZ Communications. We all called him Old John behind his back.

Old John came from Taiwan. In discussions he was always very serious and engaged, as if he had never left school. His face must have been very handsome in his youthful days. Traces of his good looks were still visible in the oblong shape of his face and his straight nose. Even now he didn't look bad at all. He wore his dense, grizzled hair side-parted, slicked back behind his ears. He never went out without getting into a well-tailored, old-styled suit with a silk kerchief tied about the collar of his shirt, in the manner of the *lao ke la*, the old classy gentlemen of old time Shanghai.

Fate wasn't exactly kind to him and one couldn't help but feel sympathy for him. Five years before, a vice president of marketing at the corporate headquarters of HZ was nearing retirement because of advanced age. When the board of directors scoured the industry for talent to replace him, their attention was drawn to Old John, who was then a vice president at SME, a competitor. When the head-hunting company hired by the board went to him to try to hire him away, Old John neither accepted nor refused the offer, which was sweetened by generous options and a salary double his present pay, but said he would consider it.

When a year later, Old John was marginalized in the aftermath of the surprisingly swift rise to power of a group of young turks at SME, he decided to accept the HZ offer. Only it was a little too late, for the vacancy left by the retired vice president had been filled at the HZ head office. In the meantime HZ Communications China, Inc. was eager to open for business but in dire need of fleshing out its high management. That was how Old John ended up becoming president of HZ Communications China. It was easy to imagine his reluctance to take the job. While he went up from vice president to become president, HZ Communications had none of the weight of the HZ parent company in the industry. That meant that when invitations to future industry summits were issued, he would probably be less likely to get one than a branch manager of the parent company, even though he was the president of HZ Communications.

The board of directors agreed that as long as Old John was willing to remain in the position at HZ Communications until retirement, the board would reward him with options, not of the subsidiary, but of the parent company at that time. In that case he would effectively return to the parent company upon retirement and would sit on its board, and would be a heavy-weight in the industry and become a permanent entry in the Who's Who of the electronic communications industry.

That was the gossip I garnered over the course of my employment at HZ Communications.

Apparently William and Old John were on quite familiar terms with each other. Often I had a hard time deciphering what they were talking about. Occasionally they would burst out laughing with knowing glances at each other over some joke, the hilarity of which was however lost on those around them.

Well, those around them meant just me and Mary, who never got into the spirit of the party and bent over her smartphone to send text messages whenever she got a chance, presumably to her nanny. Tonight she had been drafted again to the dinner party and was taken away from her Dongdong.

Mary had a fairer complexion than most women. In happy moments, her white complexion would be tinged with rosiness, but when she was tense or sad, it would take on a bluish tint. While she did not have the healthy-looking, smooth and fine skin of Jessica, there was a special kind of delicate and sensitive beauty about Mary. She had uncreased eyelids and a straight nose and lips that were always ever so lightly pressed together. Deep down she must be a quiet and discreet person. Perhaps feeling out of her element in the department, she often spoke in a tentative, uneasy voice, which tended to become increasingly tenuous until it became inaudible at the end of her sentence. What enlivened her face were the two disproportionately large front teeth that were half revealed whenever she smiled. They evoked the image of a timid, cute little white rabbit.

William liked to tease Old John for being a henpecked husband who so feared his wife that in all the years when his wife and daughter stayed faraway in the United States he still dreaded taking an escort girl out. Holding a glass of wine in his hand, Old John facetiously shook his head and sighed and leaned over to whisper something into William's ear. It sounded like he was wary of what the police of mainland China might do in that case.

"You are wrong, you are wrong," William said, waving a hand dismissively before suddenly shouting out, "Mary, have I invited you here to eat, or to send text messages? Well, get over here and have a drink!"

Old John did have an impressive capacity for alcohol! I was already half drunk as a result of clinking glasses with him, when he only started to show signs of slackening. William prodded

Mary to drink three rounds of three cups each to Old John. Clearly little able to hold her drink, Mary forced down the first three cups with a rigidity of gesture that came from anger she had to suppress because it was bad form to make a scene on such an occasion. With the fourth cup, she already showed signs of going into a stupor. Soon she was to take the sixth drink.

Old John had sat in the honor seat, with me and William placed next to him on both side, and Mary opposite us. William left his seat and made Mary take his seat while he sat down on the other side of her. "There's no fun in drinking like that," he said. "With the remaining three cups, let's throw dices. Whoever loses drinks one. How about that?"

The two dice cups containing six dice each were flipped over to rest on the table. Old John waved a hand in a gentlemanly manner to indicate that the lady should go first. Mary managed to scatter the dice all over the floor in the first try. Old John, clearly a pro, flexed his wrist to move the cup in a grinding pattern. As the cup was almost lifted off the surface of the table, the dice kept rolling inside. Three 2's, four 2's, three 3's, four 3's, five 3's. Slightly inebriated and still feeling upset and in an urge to win, she called time and again only to find she had misjudged. Old John, obviously a little embarrassed by his winning streak, deliberately lost to Mary a few times and drank up for her. The three remaining cups were long gone, but Mary was loath to give up yet and Old John was just beginning to enjoy the game. Thus the seesawing went on and penalty drinks were downed by one or the other in a seemingly never-ending game.

I wasn't sure if my eyes were playing tricks on me, but William's chair seemed to be nudging closer and closer toward Mary. This caused Mary to move closer to Old John without realizing it herself and as they guessed at the points of the dice, their knees nearly touched. Whenever she guessed wrong, Mary drank with increasing abandon, shooting to her feet, throwing her head back to down the drink as if wishing to kill herself on the spot with some poison. Before she had a chance to sit down,

William gave her a push, sending her stumbling into the lap of Old John.

The unsuspecting Old John caught her in her fall, but his arms froze because he didn't have the strength to pull her up, nor did he have the temerity to let the momentum of her fall send her straight into his arms. But they were in fact in each other's arms, with Mary's elbows on Old John's chest and her knees landing between his thighs. She gave a short, sharp cry, with confusion in her eyes, as if puzzled by the posture she found herself in. When she tried to straighten up by supporting herself on something, she found that whether she accomplished that by using her hands or her legs, she would cause her body to have more points of contact with Old John's body. Abruptly sobering up she frantically twisted around and, with one hand, gripped the table as support, knocking over two glasses of wine in the process, spilling a full glass of liquor on her and on Old John's legs. With a cry, Old John pushed Mary away to salvage his suit.

If I were Mary, I would have given William a slap on the face the moment I got up off the carpeted floor. But, would I really? I asked myself. Mary merely stared at William with fury in her eyes, while William pretended the whole thing had nothing to do with him. "Ah yah! How did this happen?" he clamored. "How did it happen!"

With a clean cloth napkin, he dabbed at the wine-stained trousers of Old John and when he was satisfied that they were relatively dry, he gave them a few extra wipes in a meaningful way, after which the two exchanged a glance and burst out laughing. With two fingers Old John lifted his still moist trouser legs and swayed. His normally serious, wooden expression was gone from his face, and in its place was an excited glow that gave the impression he had just come off a Shoot the Chute ride.

They retrieved the dice cups and the dice that had been scattered onto the carpeted floor in Mary's struggle but two dice remained missing after much searching. "Why don't you two go on betting on something else," William said. Then he turned around and asked me, "Do you know some other game?"

I gave a perfunctory answer. "How about finger guessing?" Nobody knew how to play it. Then I said, "How about rock-paper-scissors?"

William clapped his hands. "This is good!"

Mary was pressed back into that same seat. She had a somber face, the alcohol almost gone from her system. Only moments before she had stood apart from the rest of us, gripping her handbag and coat all set to leave. She told me later that rock-paper-scissors was a game she often played with Dongdong.

After drinking another three cups, she called out, "Rock, paper, scissors!" She started raising her hand when she suddenly drew it back and began sobbing into her hands until she buried her head into her folded arms and cried now with a vengeance. As she wept with an utter abandonment, her shoulders convulsed uncontrollably. The fit of crying killed the mood around the table and a disgusted William said with a frown, "She's drunk."

I hurried over to the cashier to settle the bill with a credit card and gave the name the receipt should be made out to.

Old John pulled his white BMW up by the curb to bid us goodbye. William went around to the front passenger side door and held opened the door. "You are in luck today," he said to Mary. "Since it was the president who got you drunk, let him make up by taking you home."

With those words he shoved Mary toward the front seat. Mary held tight to the door, adamantly refusing to get in. Old John stuck out his head. "Let her be, let her be!"

"I'll take her home," I immediately said. William thrust her toward me and laughed. "She has spoiled the fun. She's all yours! I'll go get my car and wash my hands of you."

The two of us were left standing in the nippy night air of early spring. The Chinese parasol trees lining the boulevard rustled in the breeze. There were a few lonely neon signs that remained lit, accentuating the quiet of the night. A line of taxis seemed to have gone to sleep. I ran over and knocked on the window on one of the waiting taxis. The driver, still drowsy, started the engine. I hastened back to Mary, who was standing near the curb, her head inclined, and her face pale, gripping the front of her blouse with one hand. She appeared to be suffering. I whispered into her ear, "There, there! The cab is here. Just hold on for a little while. You will be home in a bit."

I held the door open but she did not budge. I was left no choice but to put my arm around her waist to try to get her into the car.

Suddenly, she slapped away my hand. "Don't touch me!"

"I didn't mean to," I said. "I didn't mean ..." Before I had time to finish the sentence, she already stumbled into the cab and slammed the door shut. With a puff of exhaust fume, the cab pulled away from where I was standing and vanished into the night.

The next morning I sat in my cubicle and kept an eye on the corridor through which every employee must pass in order to reach the time clock to punch in. At 8:50, Mary still hadn't shown up, as she normally did. I had found out she always arrived for work earlier than most only because I happened to come to the office early a few times. Nine, five past nine, then half past nine, and there was still no sign of her frail figure.

What trouble did Mary get into? Did she fall ill because she had had too much to drink? Or did her son have some kind of accident the night before because he was left unattended? Whatever happened, how could she cope alone? Everyone at the office knew that Mary was divorced. She had worked previously at MG and was Jessica's colleague in the PR department there. She resigned in order to devote herself to carrying her baby to term. She never suspected that her husband had been carrying on with another woman during her pregnancy. The moment her child turned three, she got a job. It was not easy for a single mother to raise a child.

On the third day Mary showed up at 8:50. Set off by the dark blue high collar knit sweater and black short coat she was wearing, her complexion looked surreally white. She must have noticed I was observing her. When she passed my cubicle, she deliberately avoided my eyes. Everything went back to normal. She turned on her computer, efficiently read and replied to emails, made phone calls and talked and laughed with self-assurance. I began to suspect that my worry had been unwarranted. Maybe she never really minded what happened a few nights before.

At ten she left her desk to make copies. It was the opportunity I had been waiting for and I picked up a few file folders at random and followed her. It was a spot near the water fountain that normally had little traffic. Outside the glass wall one could see the parking lot below.

I went up to her and asked in a low voice, "Are you okay?"

The beam of light from the scanning lamp of the copier swept across her face back and forth, like a searchlight moving across a stone statue. The question once asked couldn't be retracted. It hung in the air, unacknowledged, so I answered my own question. "If you don't like drinking at dinner parties, you don't have to in the future."

She abruptly turned around to face me, her face even paler than before and the look in her eyes razor-sharp. "Do I have a choice?" she asked. "It doesn't cost you anything to give that advice, but can you really refuse to drink in a situation like that?"

I was at a loss to answer her and was a little crestfallen. "Mary, I said all that only because I care about you. I ..."

"Oh, thank you very much!" Mary said in a shrill voice. "When you first came to the company, I watched how they ganged up to try to get you drunk. I was worried about you then. It never occurred to me that you were just like them. You enjoy that kind of thing!"

My face turned crimson. Thomas chose this moment to make his way to the copier with a bunch of files. He was startled by the expression on my face but greeted me as if he had noticed nothing. "Boss, just leave your documents with me. I'll do them for you. I have a lot to copy myself so I'll just wait in line here."

Mary pulled out the last page of her document out of the copier. The edge of the A4 paper glinted in the sun, a sharp knife that silently broke the continuity of the air. With a blank look in her eyes, a spring in her step, and calm composure she turned around and left holding between her fingers the originals and the copies in two separate stacks. You would think she never uttered a word and that serene expression on her face never changed.

At this moment my feet were heading to the copier, but my mind was telling me to run after Mary and clarify things once and for all. My right foot managed to step on the toes of my left foot. With a grimace and a frown, I tried to decide which document I should pull out from the stack held in my left arm and my right hand hesitated in the air. Then I gave the copier an unreasonably wide berth, mumbling a string of sounds unintelligible even to myself. As Thomas nodded in feigned understanding, I made my way back toward the office in a weaving manner with his eyes following me like a spotlight.

Soon it was lunch time. When I insinuated myself into the crowded elevator, the overcapacity alarm went off and I had to beat a shame-faced retreat. Gripped by a sudden urge to stay as far away as possible from the milling humanity on this floor, I turned about and walked to the nearest exit. I pushed open the metal door and walked eleven floors down. Never before had I, with my corpulence and low energy, chosen the stairs over the elevator.

In sharp contrast to the well-appointed office space, the fire escape stairwell was dark, stark, narrow, deserted, and even a little run-down. My lonely footsteps echoed between the grimy tiled surfaces. It was there that I ran into Mary again, a dark blue figure, long hair tied into a bun, and a white-complexioned side of her face flashed before my eyes as she made a turn in the staircase. I ran after her.

I called after her, "Mary, wait for me. Listen to what I have to say!"

"Mary, if I am not the kind of person you thought I was,

then what kind of person am I?" I said. "Well, it's hard to make you understand in a few words. You'll understand as time goes on. What I wanted to say is, Mary, if there's any social activity of the department that you'd rather not join, you don't have to. I'll ask William to exempt you!"

There was a blank look on Mary's face and she didn't slow down, but neither did she exhibit the kind of hostility she adopted toward me earlier that morning. With her hands in her coat pockets, she said dismissively, "You'll do that for me? Do you really believe you can accomplish that?"

My generous impulse choked for a brief moment in the throat of reality, but my answer was as fast as the momentum of my descending steps. "Of course I can!"

Mary did not change her pace as she said casually, as if of some trivial matter, "You must have heard about what happened to Rita. I'm not like her. I have a kid. Dongdong has nobody but me to count on, so I can't afford to lose this job. Do you understand now?"

I had never seen Rita, who had left before I reported to the marketing department. The official version was that Rita failed the annual performance appraisal of the personnel department and had tendered her resignation after William had a talk with her. But another scenario was bruited about in the grapevine. In this version of the story, Rita graduated from Columbia University summa cum laude, had short hair and long legs, and was very capable and proud. She never deigned to attend any of William's dinner parties, nor any drinking party with Old John present. It was also rumored that the infamous annual performance appraisal report was personally penned by William and signed by Old John.

I realized that Mary did not believe I was capable of protecting her, that she even doubted my sincerity. She mentioned Rita as a subtle way to advise me not to promise more I could deliver, and not to risk the livelihood of a single mother like her just for the sake of feeling good.

Hah! Was I such a person? After feeling upset for a while, I realized that I was indeed such a person. But then I immediately came up with a counter-argument. Who says I was just bluffing? Who says I can't get William to permit Mary to absent herself from the parties? I am after all William's pal now. He has even asked me to call him Will and if I didn't call him Will, he would punish me by forcing me to drink a cup of liquor.

That thought bolstered me up. "Mary, I don't care what you think of me. But I've decided to take you into my charge. Next time William has a dinner party, you don't say anything to his face. You just go home after work and leave the rest to me. I will take care of the matter for you."

In my excitement, I added for good measure, "Mary, why do you always care about what people think and appear to be so tensed? Why don't you relax and be yourself as you do now? See? You look so good when you relax!"

In the flight after flight of stairs, our footsteps echoed in the quiet of the stairwell as we walked down one behind the other, our paces gradually coming in sync with only half a beat's difference in the rhythms of our steps. Whenever I rounded the bend to the next flight of stairs, she would also take on her next flight. I had only the time during five or six steps to have a view of her below me, after which she would be hidden by the handrail and would come back into my view at her next change of flights. When I finished my little speech, my view of her was blocked by the handrail and the only response I heard was the hollow sound of treading.

A sense of unease arose in me. Could what I said have made her despise me even more? At a turning I suddenly saw her stop in the middle of the flight to look up at me. That brief meeting of our eyes was accompanied by a soft twitch of a corner of her mouth. I could see the return to her eyes the look of friendliness and trust that she used to reserve for me, only mixed now with a tinge of contrition. Tilting her head at that angle to look up at me, she reminded me of a demure flower turned toward the sun.

That was the Mary I was familiar with, the person that all this time I had cared about without realizing it, that I had meant to protect.

But it was at that instant that I was struck by a fear. I had not expected that it was so easy to assume a burden. What was most risible was the fact that I had arrogated to myself the role of her protector against William with a confidence that was based on my belief that William considered me a pal—a basis that recalled the fabled ass in the lion's skin.

It so happened that the very next day William organized another dinner party at Xianghuqing Restaurant, to which all staff members in the marketing department were invited. Half an hour before the office closed, Mary quietly readied her handbag, which she laid at the foot of her chair, and looked over her shoulder at me. To her querying look I could only respond with an affirmative nod and a smile signifying everything's under control. I watched as she quietly shut down her computer, picked up her handbag, and disappeared behind the closing door of the elevator, leaving an empty chair which I'd have to explain to William.

William was careful to spare my sensibilities. "Kevin, oh Kevin, it was just that one night for the two of you," he said with a slight frown and an arching of eyebrows. "Do you mean to tell me that after just one night, you've become her guardian?"

I could detect an effort to suppress anger on his part. The most practical response at a moment like this would be to immediately follow that up with unsparing self-mockery and the promise of not repeating the offence in the future. But somehow his vulgar imagination breached the limits of my patience. "We are not that sordid."

I could see his face flush with fury, but only for a moment. Carefully and with an expression frozen at the moment of changing, he examined me. "Kevin, what's the matter with you?"

I hastened to explain haltingly. "I've probably had too much to drink these days and hurt my liver. That's why I have mood swings." I then added, "Will, I am only asking you to cut some slack for Mary, seeing that she has a tough time bringing up a child all by herself. Besides, she just can't cut it when it comes to drinking, so she really doesn't contribute much to dinner parties anyway."

Backing down meant that I had no ace up my sleeve, and that I was merely temporarily out of control. That was the cue for William to unleash his fury on me. "In my department you don't play big daddy protecting someone!" he said, pointing his finger at my nose. "You'd be lucky to get your own work done!"

He huffed and puffed around the desk. I remained silent and standing at attention, unsure where to rest my eyes. After a while, he seemed to come to a decision to let me off the hook this time. "I'm warning you. Only this once! If you ask me for leave again on her behalf, I'll give both of you a very long leave of absence!" Then he pointed at the windbreaker hanging on the coat rack. "What are you standing there for? Don't you see it's time the party started?"

I unhooked the windbreaker and draped it respectfully over my arm and followed him out of his office. The other staff in the department judged by the fact that we came out of the manager's office together that my friendship with him must have grown by leaps and bounds. Therefore they all vied to flash a friendly smile at me. The entire department, carrying a case of raspberry vodka, descended in the elevator, walked out of the building, turned right, and entered once again that private banquet room redolent of roast fish.

I phoned Jessica. I never suspected that I would so soon consent to be a spy, not for lucre or the prospect of a promotion up the corporate ladder, nor for revenge or justice, but because of a pressing need to face an impending crisis. How would I ask William again for leave on behalf of Mary with the next dinner party looming and how would I deliver on my promise to Mary?

Clearly my thinking through and accepting her offer so soon caught Jessica by surprise. Her startled tone in the first two or three minutes of our phone conversation caused my cheeks to burn and my voice to drop almost into a whisper. After I managed to finish my rambling account, I sensed a hesitation at Jessica's end before she spoke up with a funny tone. "Is that all?"

"That's all," I answered in embarrassment.

I heard a noise which sounded as if Jessica was switching her phone to the other ear. Then she resumed in her usual even and soft voice. "Kevin, do I have to remind you that even if William uses his office as the manager of his department to compel his subordinates to participate in dinner parties against their will and forced them to drink alcohol, there's no way to prove it and anyway it's no big deal. Besides, is it work-related? Has he violated any company rules? Do you really think Carl can take action against him on that basis alone? I have business to attend to at the moment. I can't continue this conversation. Put your mind to finding his work-related missteps. We will discuss how to deal with him when you find something more damnable to hold against him."

"Wait!" I was desperate to prevent Jessica from hanging up, but was at a loss to find in a pinch anything more damnable, so I grabbed at any straw that came within reach. "You know, William seems to be on intimate terms with Old John."

Jessica's answer came fast. "We knew that. They have always belonged to the same faction."

I was again casting about for a subject, but the jabs that I threw seemed to lack punch. "William is a pander for Old John. He set up Old John with female colleagues of the department, who wined and dined Old John and even came close to offering other services."

Jessica interrupted my stuttering account. "Kevin, I told you already, all that is of no use to us. There's no need to rush. Spend more time to find some actionable information. It can wait a few days."

I thought to myself that in those few days William might again demand Mary's attendance at one of his dinner parties.

How would I keep my promise to Mary? I was on the point of saying something when Jessica suddenly changed back to her funny tone. "Kevin, are you dating Mary?"

I hastened to clarify. "I am not only speaking for Mary. As I said, there are other victims in the marketing department."

"Is that so?" Jessica said. "How come I am unaware of any complaints? I have the impression that they all enjoy that with William."

Suddenly a name popped into my mind and I grasped at the straw. "Rita! You should have seen her, right? Everybody at the marketing department knows that William did something with her annual performance appraisal and compelled her to resign because of her refusal to participate in the dinner parties."

"Hmm, that sounds more interesting, if we can get real proof."

Yes, I was a spy in the marketing department. Whatever the value of the information I gathered, I had become a threat planted by Jessica in the proximity of William. My exile was a correct decision by William, who wanted me away from the marketing department, away from Shanghai and maybe even out of this life completely. In that case I would become a mere statistic in a report of an unsolved case shelved in some police station.

IX

Spring came to Shucun village, a mistimed celebration in my circumstance. The sunlight became warmer and the air was laden with greater moisture, generating mists and fogs that veiled the surrounding mountains, turning it greener by the day. The Jinsha River, like a soft, flowing band of silk, sent off muted glitters as scudding light clouds cast their shadows on the earth. On this cinquefoil of a plain—this jail cage of mine—thousands of wild flower species had burst into bloom in every corner in resplendent clusters.

I had the strangest of sensation. I had lost everything, was all alone and friendless, with, constantly hanging over my head, the Damocles sword of death by a sharp knife and sacrifice to the gods. I felt like a lone passenger standing on the deck of a sinking ship. And yet my body was basking in the glory of this beautiful weather. I didn't need any reason other than the mere contact of my skin with the air to feel a burgeoning sense of happiness.

In the aftermath of my failed attempt to escape, Shuren did not tie a rope to my legs or attach a bell to my neck. Needless to say, his forgiveness did not stop me from planning my escape, only whenever I went out I would explain to him sheepishly I was going out to collect some firewood, or I was going to gather some wild fruits.

I was in fact trying to find that trail that would lead me out of captivity. Mr. Liu said that there was only one road linking Shucun with the outside world and you couldn't miss it. That would mean that if I found where that road ended in Shucun, I could run from that point and would return without fail to the point of the car accident, without having to worry about getting lost in the jungle covering the mountains. Once I was back on the trunk road, my return to the civilized world would be a real possibility.

I planned to reconnoiter with care the outer periphery of the plain. To accomplish that undertaking, I estimated that I would need about two weeks. For one thing it was a huge plain and I had no transportation, not even a bicycle. I also needed to break up the project into several separate casual trips for each of which I needed to invent some kind of excuse, such as stumbling upon a pile of dried twigs and pieces of firewood, or my attention suddenly being drawn to a grove of trees laden with fruit.

I mustn't walk too fast. I had to make frequent resting stops and sometimes retrace my steps a bit, as if I had no pre-planned route, otherwise it wouldn't take long before the villagers saw through my purpose. When I was sure they were no longer looking at me, I'd immediately break into a brisk walk and even run in quick, short steps, just to speed up the anemic progress of my investigations.

In order to complete my project at an early date, I forced myself to rise early so that I could have more time for my forays. I made a point of sleeping in a corner of the big house with the largest number of cracks in the wall. When the first points of light fell on my eyelids, I would force open my eyes and spring up with a show of reinvigorated energy. On my Longines Master Collection chronograph dial watch that survived the crash, the hands would normally indicate 5 AM at this point. The sky would be half mellow yellow and half dark blue with a pale moon.

Luckily, Shuren was an even earlier riser. By the time I woke up, he was already walking back at a leisurely pace, his footfalls crisp with dew. He heaved the small basket off his back and picked out the blades of grass and pieces of tree roots he had just collected. The Bull Bear shifted its body in the darkness, and turned its face toward the light of the breaking day. Occasionally its eyes the size of tennis balls would sneak a glance at me and wink naughtily as Shuren put the morning's harvest into the pot and started to make his concoction, as if saying to me, "Ugh, not that yucky medicinal brew again!"

Shuren's feet always landed softly and imperturbably as he went about his daily tasks in a routine that differed little from day to day, preparing medicinal brews, making tea and baking flat bread, and of course burning incense, mixing colors and painting gods and ghosts, which was his specialty. He even possessed a complete set of wooden printing blocks carved with fine patterns; he would apply a specially made dark ink over one of those blocks and cover it with cloths already cut to size to produce in one afternoon a large number of prayer flags.

I would feign enthusiasm and ask with the help of gestures. "Is there anything I can do to help?"

Shuren would invariably lift his eyes narrowed by a smile to look at me and shrug his shoulders, as if embarrassed by my offer.

I would then pick up another back basket behind the door and point at the outdoors. I would enact a mime indicating that I was going to fill up the basket with something and would then hastily step out with the old man looking after me with his forever smiling eyes.

Shuren didn't need me to collect firewood. Early every morning, neatly stacked firewood would materialize behind the house and water from the brook would fill the water vats under the eaves. Shuren had a son by the name of Ah Rong who didn't live in the big house but a number of houses down. He had a complexion as dark as rye and bright eyes. His braided hair was tied into a neat coil on top of his head. He had wide shoulders and narrow hips, an unusually thick neck, and strong jawbone. If I were a city girl I would scream with thrill at the sight of this man.

The firewood he delivered was all from the best tree trunks, split into segments of equal size with a hatchet. Unlike his father, he moved with agility and recklessness and was fleet of feet. He was said to be the second best hunter in the village. I imagined he must have chopped all that wood stacked against the mud wall all the way to the top with the same ease with which a chef diced his tofu. He would never have stooped to pick up the kind of dried twigs and dead leaves that served as a lame excuse for my secret missions of reconnaissance.

But when I returned at noon time and poured out the measly content of my little back basket and placed it beside the fire pit where Shuren had his usual seat, he would look at it with an unfailing look of approval and move his hands over it, smiling and shaking his head. At first I thought the shaking of his head signified bitter disappointment, but I found out later that whenever he showed appreciation for something he would accompany his smile with a habitual shaking of his head, which translated into something like "this is the best."

According to the date dial on my Longines chronograph, I spent all of twelve days to accomplish the covert mission of canvassing the terrain around the village (I wonder if the attempt at covertness had the opposite effect). I carefully cased the entire periphery of the village without finding the trail that led to the outside world. I saw nothing resembling a point of entry into the village. In all directions there was nothing but mountains, forests, clouds and fogs, and variegated wild flowers of multiple colors.

I found that I did not need to camouflage my intentions by punctuating my hikes with rest stops or taking circuitous routes or detours, for nobody was observing me. People went about their own business, too absorbed in what they were doing to notice even an important prisoner like me. Their dedication astonished me. It was a dedication that I had never come across in the office through my entire career. In contrast to these primitive villagers, my previous colleagues, who performed mental labor, could type the word dedication on their keyboard but beyond that knew practically nothing about dedication. The villagers were so dedicated to their respective work that it almost seemed that work was their only raison d'être.

As day broke, men carried water, made tea, and women prepared meals. Smoke from the cooking fires curled up from the glistening roofs of the village, creating a mass that slowly rose to become one with the clouds. When the smoke dissipated, men set out toward the barns on the hills or the periphery of Shucun village to start working the fields opened up by the villagers. The women stayed behind to work outside their own homes. This would go on until the sun was overhead. People would pass the quiet afternoon maintaining a deliberate but steady pace of work. Then, always at a fixed point of time, Shuren would emerge from the big house and in front of the house with his face turned toward the west he would start to chant in his husky and lilting voice. *Jia-luo-ni-jia-yeh, mo-lo-mo-lo.* As if by tacit accord, as the soughing among the trees followed the blowing of the wind, everyone—on hills, in the fields, in front of houses—in an area of several square kilometers—stopped what they were doing and drew themselves up, turned in the direction of the setting sun and started chanting. *Jia-luo-ni-jia-yeh, mo-lo-mo-lo* ...

A fixed point of time may not sound very precise. This point of time came every day about dozens of breaths before the sun sank behind the mountain ridge. But the hands on my watch seemed indifferent to the pace at which the sun moved in its trajectory. As I observed the sun's never-changing daily routine from this remote corner of the world, I read a completely different time on the dial of my watch. I no longer knew which time to follow.

As for those two sentences that they chanted daily, my guess was they were words of prayer. The villagers didn't seem to have much use for any form of currency, so they presumably did not pray for lucre, or for a good job, or a successful professional career, an early appointment to the position of branch manager, or a transfer to the corporate headquarters. Since they made such a fuss over their crops every day, I could only guess they were praying for a good harvest.

I couldn't have been more wrong as it turned out later.

One day, Shuren told me what those sentences meant: "Thank you! See you tomorrow!"

"Thank who?" I asked.

Shuren said with a laugh and a shake of his head, "We have so much to be thankful for. The sun shines on the earth for a good part of the day. We want to thank it for its hard work and generosity and pray that it will come calling again tomorrow morning. The ancestors of the bears have blessed this plain for another day. We thank them for accepting our forefathers and thank them and their descendants for their acceptance and amicability and pray that come tomorrow morning this land will still be blessed with peace and harmony as it has been in the past millennium. We also thank the Jinsha River for irrigating this land for yet another day, and we hope that tomorrow morning it will continue to run clear and strong without cease."

Several years after these words from Shuren, weather suddenly became for the first time a major topic that got the attention of office animals. The planet was rocked by one earthquake after another and volcanic eruptions, throwing up volcanic ashes that blocked the sky and the sun and grounded aeronautic wonders. In the north, snow and sleet persisted in late May. The southeast was hit by sandstorms, the west by cyclones and the southwest suffered from severe drought followed by disastrous floods.

Before this, as with most civilized people, my first reaction would have been what is there to be thankful for in all that? The sun always rises every day without fail. How can a river suddenly dry up? As for bears, they should thank their lucky stars if they are not hunted down by humans who sell bear paws and bear gall bladders for a hefty profit.

Interestingly, we city people religiously pay our water, gas, and phone bills for fear of having our electricity or water cut off or losing the dial tone when we pick up our phone next month for nonpayment. In order to pay these daily expenses, we must punch in at our workplace, get in the good graces of our bosses and make an effort to socialize with clients and associates. We are always busy keeping up this rat race, this game of catchup, living from hand to mouth in this man-made world, while we take for granted gifts of nature, such as the sun and the air we breathe, or even forget they are there. Or do we really believe that we—poor creatures who have no control over our own lives—are the masters that control everything?

I struggled with these thoughts. One moment there was certainty, the next moment I was confused again.

Shuren watched, asking no questions and offering no clarifications. "You are not from Shucun, so you don't need to observe our customs," he said. "One day, when you heart is ready, you will offer thanks of your own accord as we do."

I began to nurse a grudge against Shuren. He never stopped me from going out to search for a route of escape. He pretended to believe my excuse of collecting firewood and at noon time he baked flat bread and left it on the stove for me. He smiled charitably at me, causing me to feel a tinge of guilt. But he must have known for a long time that this prisoner of his was never going to make it out of this plain.

I did another round of reconnaissance on the edges of the village. This time I made good progress because I didn't have to hide my purpose. It took me only nine days. But that legendary trail connecting the village to the outside world still eluded me. Not ready to take defeat lying down, I started all over again, a third time and then a fourth.

I alternated between despair, anxiety, and a vague expectation. I couldn't help wondering in a world without me, who would still think of me at this moment and persist in an effort to find me despite the total lack of any clues to my fate and whereabouts? Would Mary, Jessica, Carl, Thomas, or William?

I watched expectantly for comings and goings of people either into or out of Shucun village. The greatest obstacle to the discovery of a way out, I found, was the fact that there was no traffic of that kind at all. On my fifth circuit around the outer limits of the plain, the picture of the world in my mind was no longer one of crisscrossing highways and stack interchanges separating blocks of highrise buildings and parking structures. Instead, I had a new perception of the world as one vast undivided land. It crested and troughed like a stirred-up sea and grew and expanded like a tree. A road is a road only if there is sustained traffic on it. It's the hastening footsteps of all those travelers that blaze a path across the land.

But in Shucun village it appeared no one had a need to travel to that outside world and no one outside of it felt the need to drop in for a visit. People waited quietly for the wheat to ripen, harvested their crop and thrashed it. With a rat–a–tat reminding one of drum rhythms, wheat kernels flew up golden and glistening in the bright sunlight and rained back down. Why indeed would they need to leave this plain?

I seemed to gradually grow out of the habit of raising my wrist to look at the watch, and of counting the hours and days. Then my Longines watch stopped ticking. It must have happened days before I noticed it. Was I being won over by this quiet, serene, and fulfilling mode of life? My corpulent body began to feel lighter. As I strolled across this beautiful plain, watching the smoke from cooking fires rise twice a day, the sun set once a day, rain alternate with shine, green wheat turn yellow, women dye and weave their yarn to make clothes, the serenity in my heart swelled until it crowded out all my confused and confusing memories.

I had frequent encounters with those bears with a human face.

They came out of hibernation in spring, still groggy from their long slumber, and moving ponderously about in the plain.

Their daily routine rather resembled that of a group of autistic humans, who slept until afternoon and began foraging for food only when daylight waned. I often wondered whether they too played games into the wee hours, only, I was afraid to venture out into the wild alone in those hours, and therefore had no way to find out.

The first time I saw a bear with a human face was by a small wooded area still lit by the low sun. It was standing almost at full height, its two paws lightly rested on the bough of a big tree, its head tilted up, chewing on the tender leaves on a side branch. It was about ten centimeters shorter than me and its mass two or three times my corpulent body. Smooth, shiny black fur covered its entire body. It had round ears and huge paws. Such a hulk was incongruously paired with a milk white face, with dumb-looking small eyes, a flat nose and mouth, and a prominent chin. The bristles that resembled sideburns bordering its cheeks accentuated its very human-like face.

In its upright posture, another feature that struck the eyes was a white streak across its chest the shape of a recumbent half-moon, which I somehow associated with a square of a white shirt peeking out of a dark suit. It stood there somewhat like a gaping corpulent white-collar office worker. Maybe that was how I had looked in my previous office existence.

Naturally, these risible thoughts were just a flash across my mind. It was my very first encounter with a bear, which were ten paces away. I almost jumped with terror. I understood only then that at a moment of absolute terror, one's hands and feet went completely numb and it was impossible to jump or flee even if one wanted to. It also spotted me at the same time and even stopped its leaf-chewing to give me a glance-over with its head tilted sideways. Its examination of me only lasted a brief moment, after which it scratched its head satisfiedly against the bough and resumed its supper, as if it had seen me before and we were on such intimate terms that all formalities such as a nod of greeting could be dispensed with. It appeared to treat me like just another bear.

With the appearance of that first bear, a "Start" button was pressed, as it were, to trigger a magic spell. From then on I suddenly began to see more and more of them, some eating berries half lying and half sitting on the grass, or leaning against some little tree hardly able to support their weight, sunning themselves, their chins smeared with purple berry juice. Some climbed up a big tree and with their chin nestled in a fork of a branch, tracked the progress of a column of ants, with their nose quivering and sniffing. Others that tried to steal honey from a hive were found out and fled through the forest to escape the pursuit of swarms of bees.

When it rained, they would often stare fixedly at a clearing in the forest despite the light drizzle and remained in that position all afternoon. Unobserved, I watched them with curiosity on several such occasions, but remained mystified about what they were doing. It was all because I had too little patience. Then one day I happened to see a young bamboo shoot slowly poke through the soil.

Then two shoots, three shoots materialized. I was rooted to the spot and couldn't move my feet, my eyes glued to those spring shoots that kept sprouting—four, then five. Like all the bears, slightly bent at the hips, I also stared fixedly at the clearing in the wood. I don't know if you've ever noticed when a shoot breaks through the ground and when it grows, it makes a sound. How should I characterize its timbre? Imagine pouring a sparkling wine from Franciacorta on the south bank of Lago D'Iseo in Lombardy, Italy, into a crystal champagne glass, lifting the icy glass to lightly touch your earlobe and closing your eyes to listen. You'll hear countless tiny air bubbles rise and break. That's the timbre of the growing sound of bamboo shoots.

Bears have poor eyesight. They are like a group of deeply nearsighted bookworms, but the round ears protruding from their heads are supersensitive to sound. Six shoots, now seven, now eight! They would cock their ears at one moment and hold them still in quiet anticipation the next, as the sound of growing bamboo shoots rises and falls.

I could see that these were timorous, emotional fellows; big and heavy as they were, they made an effort to tread and move lightly. They were clunky but sensitive and introverted; they preferred peace and quiet and easily got nervous and they were almost all herbivores. Perhaps as a result of their flat mouth and prominent jaw, which stood out more than their forehead, they appeared to permanently wear a faint, timid and bashful smile, if our understanding of human facial expressions could apply to them.

After my arrival at Shucun village, I began for the first time to doubt the knowledge drilled into our head about animals. I wondered why human society branded many animals as "ferocious beasts" and then taught us that they drank blood, were born enemies of humans, hurt and devoured people, and therefore we must fear them and fight and kill them with all weapons available to us. Of humans and these animals, which should more appropriately be called "ferocious beasts" and which should fear the other more?

The Shucun villagers were expert hunters, but they strictly followed a set of hunting rules. They could only hunt on designated dates. Not everyone could go on a hunt; "hunters" were special people selected by the Elder. Besides being strong of body, they had to have a knack for detecting changes in the clouds, the sun and the wind, and a knowledge of animal habits, and they must take a solemn oath to adhere to the principles of being a "hunter."

"What are the principles involved in being a 'hunter'?" I asked Ah Rong, son of Shuren.

Ah Rong laughed. "There are too many to explain in a few words." We chatted as he carried the threshed wheat to the big house. While his command of Han Chinese was much worse than Shuren's, we still managed to talk for a long time with the help of gestures. When he saw Shuren coming toward the big house, he quickly ended our conversation and got ready to skedaddle. I wondered if all adult sons avoided speaking to their father and Shucun was no exception.

Shuren asked Ah Rong to stay for dinner. Ah Rong pointed outdoors as though he still had a lot to attend to, and then he hurried out. "When you come with us on our next hunting trip, you'll understand." Those were his partying words to me.

At these words, Shuren gave him a sharp look, but it was wasted on him because Ah Rong was already at a great distance, his glistening muscular back disappearing in the sunlit field.

Shuren was said to have opposed Ah Rong's becoming a hunter. The office of the Elder was a hereditary one and therefore Ah Rong had no choice but to learn mantra chanting, casting of spells, the art of divination, of healing and the practice of presiding over rites of worship, marriages and funerals, hunting and the slaughter of animals. But Ah Rong exhibited an extraordinary talent for hunting at an early age. Before the rite of passage that signaled the entry into adulthood, every youngster in Shucun had to learn how to survive in the wild and be put through real tests. It was then that Ah Rong already proved far superior to his coevals in survival skills. According to the custom of hunter selection, at every rite of initiation into adulthood, a new hunter would be picked from among the initiates, and he was without a doubt the first choice.

There was nothing for Shuren but to comfort himself with the thought that sacrificial rites and killing of game were a little like father and son—they are opposites but at the same time one comes from the other. Besides, the road to the office of Elder was long and Ah Rong was still young; there might yet be time to temper his rock-hard heart and temperament in the course of hunting game. He little expected that in the seven years since Ah Rong became the second best hunter in the village, his interest in learning the practice of sacrificial rites dwindled even further.

The number one hunter in Shucun was none other than the

village chief Aqingbu. As explained by Shuren, the Elder was responsible for matters concerning gods and spirits, while the village chief was in charge of human affairs. They complemented each other in this division of labor. As for the relative weight of the two, Shuren refrained from any comment; but judging by the different attitudes of the villagers toward Shuren and Aqingbu, I could guess the answer to that.

Aqingbu's physique drew comparisons with bears. He was stout and bulky, had big strong hands and feet. Small in stature yet of prepossessing girth, he dwarfed the muscular Ah Rong, who would appear slender when placed next to him. Aqingbu's heavy-set physique encouraged me to imagine that he would not necessarily be the loser in a fight with a bear. He was darker than many of the villagers in complexion, which was a copper that gleamed in the blazing sun. There was always a glimmer of laughter in the pair of small eyes, which burned with confidence between two prominent cheeks.

He was on familiar terms with everybody in the village, clapping them on the shoulder, exchanging snuff, as if he were every man's brother. When he ran into someone on the road, he would often ease the back basket off that person's back and casually sling it over his own shoulder and walk and chat with him for part of the way.

Shuren was also congenial and easygoing and not given to putting on airs, but everybody stopped reverentially at a distance upon seeing him and would wait until he had conveyed friendly greetings before moving on. People seemed normally more inclined to chat with Aqingbu than with Shuren, but when there was a death in the family or some other misfortune or trouble, they would only go to Shuren.

People came to the big house to seek Shuren's advice on all kinds of questions they had about their daily or inner life. When the session was over, they backed out of the door and turned their back only after they were outside. Aqingbu observed the same formality when he came to discuss village matters. There were only two people who did not follow the rule; one was Ah Rong, who always bolted out of his father's house faster than a rabbit. I was the other exception. As a prisoner, I was exempted from following the rules binding on a villager.

My eagerness for a chance to go on one of their hunts actually did not arise from a wish to be enlightened about the principles of being a "hunter." Given that my search for an escape route was going nowhere, following them on their outing would represent my best hope of scouting out this route. A few weeks later an officially sanctioned hunting day finally came around. To my surprise Shuren categorically rejected my request to join the hunting party.

"This is a dangerous activity," he said.

I hastened to assure him. "I know. I will not poke around, provoking wild animals. I will keep close to the hunting party."

Shuren said: "That's not what I meant. I'm not worried about wild animals hurting you. I can treat any physical injuries you might suffer. But if your inner demons break loose, it's going to be a big problem." But, Shuren said, although he couldn't take me hunting with him, he could tell me what the principles of being a "hunter" were.

According to the laws of Shucun village, a hunting party must be accompanied by the Elder. They set off before sunrise and in preparation for the hunt in the mountains they smeared their whole body with a biological powder emitting a special scent. This powder called *suma* could allegedly prevent inner demons from being unleashed. Another practical purpose of the fragrant powder was to alert their neighbors the "bears with a human face." The bears' poor eyesight was compensated for by an acute sense of smell and hearing; the fragrance acted as a sort of friendly warning to the bears: Sorry for the disturbance. To avoid accident injury, please stay clear of us.

Sentinels, drivers, attackers and blockers were deployed in the hunt, which was normally restricted to a designated area, to narrow the scope of disturbance to the forests, and to prevent excessive wounding of animals at the expense of actual game harvested. There were iron-clad rules that could not be circumvented. For instance, gravely wounded animals must be hunted down and killed to spare them a slow, painful death in the wild and to prevent wounded beasts in frantic flight from injuring people working in the fields or cutting wood in the forest. It was not allowed to harm animals younger than a year old, even though these tasted better and were easy to hunt. Nor were the hunters allowed to hurt maternal animals that were either pregnant or had young ones to care for.

There must be no hatred. The law of the jungle, a system in which the strongest survive, is a law of nature. What drives it is not hatred, but all life's need to grow. There were instances of feral beasts killing Shucun villagers who went into the mountains to gather wood, but this was no reason for hunters to single out those animals and try to exterminate them, just as wild animals would see nothing unusual in the hunting and killing of animals at designated times and within set limits.

Hunters must not go exclusively for big game to prove their bravery to their peers. Nor were they allowed to indulge the habit of bullying the weak by exclusively hunting down small animals. All animals were equal. When a hunter saw a larger animal pursue a smaller one, he must not come to the rescue of the latter with his arrows out of a naïve compassion, for this would upset the normal order of the jungle. A hunter should not be greedy. The success of a hunt must not be equated to the maximum amount of game that could be harvested but the right amount. The game harvested on each hunting expedition should be just enough to supply fifty-four households with a portion of fresh game meat each. In the next hunt, the harvest would go to another fifty-four households. In this way all two hundred seventy-two households of the village would get their share of fresh game meat in five hunting expeditions. Any animal hunted above that amount would be another life lost for no good purpose.

And what was Shuren's role in the hunt? "A hunting expedition is an event comparable in gravitas to rituals of divine worship, exorcism of evil spirits, marriages, funerals and births," Shuren explained. "It involves a symbiosis between humans and their neighbors; humans must foster this relationship with dignity and ritual correctness." Whenever an animal was killed, Shuren would immediately chant a mantra to allow its soul to depart in peace.

Shuren's tirade sorely tried my patience. So what if I found peace and quiet in this Shangri-La of a place and my stay here was relaxing physically and mentally? I couldn't very well stay here forever, could I? Shuren's refusal to take me on the hunting expedition rankled in my heart.

On the day of the hunt, I was left behind to man the fort in the big house. In the quiet afternoon I vaguely heard a weathered voice chanting at a great distance: "*Hu-ma-hu-ma-la-ni-yeh, hu-ma-hu-ma-ge-la-jia.*" It was the gentle, sandpapery voice of Shuren. Why did I have a sense of having heard this singing voice before? Then the penny dropped: about two months before, when I was carried on a pole into the village, I heard that same faraway chanting. Now I understood that Shuren was sending the soul of a slain animal on its way.

Those two short months felt like a lifetime to me.

I was alone with the Bull Bear in the big house. It had borne its injuries stoically, sprawled on a hemp mat inside, cut off from sunlight all these days and months. It had an erratic appetite; when it felt reasonably well, it would lap up two or three bowls of honey, eat a few fresh, tender bamboo shoots and a plate of nandina berries, and that was the limit. Occasionally it ate a small amount of dried fish but would never touch smoked meat. When it didn't feel so well, it would forgo food the whole day, and sometimes it would cough up dark blood. Despite the fatigue, pain and irritability that must certainly accompany this bedridden life, it kept its unshakable equanimity and that innocent gleam in its clear eyes with which it listened to people talk or watched their comings and goings. This only deepened my guilt.

Twice a day it meekly drank up the medicinal brew prepared by Shuren, even on days when it couldn't stomach a sip of honey. I could see the herbs collected every morning by Shuren change as the weeks went by and the dosage increase. The recovery of the Bull Bear from its injuries was fitful. There were periods when it would try earnestly to struggle to its feet, its paws clawing noisily on the floor; then all of a sudden it would slump down in resignation, with its chin resting on the floor, its skin burning and sweating under its fur in a low-grade fever, quivering with every breath.

At dusk the hunting party returned with a wild boar, which would improve the diet of one fifth of the villagers while the other four fifths would have to wait for future hunting expeditions. Crinkling his eyes in a broad smile, Shuren handed me a bowl of meat, which out of peeve I had wanted to refuse, but the aroma was simply too tempting. I got up, grabbed the bowl and went to sit on the threshold and started feeding it into my mouth with an eager hand.

Two days later when Shuren had left to collect herbs and I was leaning against the pile of firewood to sneak a moment of indolence, I suddenly became aware of a tapping on the wooden wall of the house: three knocks followed by a pause then another three knocks. It appeared to be intended for me. Then I saw Ah Rong wave to me by the water vat behind the house. Obviously he had just filled the vat and had struck the wall with the pole for carrying the water buckets to signal me to come out.

With a mysterious air and a finger to his lips, he cautioned me against making a noise, although he couldn't suppress a chuckle himself. "Haven't you always wanted to go on a hunt with us? Let's go, now!"

Before I had time to remind him that it was not an officially sanctioned hunting day, Ah Rong already dragged me away.

We circled around the back of a cluster of houses. The morning fog had not yet dissipated and it was still dark; our tread on the bedewed grass made a crunching sound. When we came to the foot of the hill, no large hunting party was in evidence; Aqingbu alone was seen pacing about a little impatiently. Slung across his shoulder were three long bows, two large cases of falcon-plumed arrows and two cloth bags.

It dawned on me that the day's hunt was not in compliance with the village laws and was done surreptitiously. But I easily overcame my hesitation, for our hunting party was a dream team! It consisted of the number one and number two hunters of Shucun village and me, and one of the three bows was prepared for me! When Aqingbu signaled me to sling the bow on my shoulder, I was overwhelmed by the privileged treatment and quickened my footsteps to catch up with them as we headed for the mountains.

I was only a prisoner, and one guilty of injuring their "bear god" in a car crash. What could be the reason for this magnanimous gesture? It was not long before a queasy feeling arose in me. It was not so long ago that the villagers thronged about me shouting: "*Xia-lu-wa, xia-lu-wa, xia-lu-wa!*" I still shuddered whenever that scene replayed in my mind. Could this be a trap? Perhaps the villagers got fed up with Shuren shielding me and had secretly entrusted Aqingbu with the nefarious task of taking me into the mountains to do me in.

Aqingbu suddenly fell in with me and clapped me on the shoulder with his huge palm and said, "I have always meant to ask was it really you who crashed into the Bull Bear with that iron-plated car of yours?"

My face turned purple before I realized it was because I had in my nervous state forgotten to breathe.

Aqingbu laughed. "Don't worry! I was only curious. I went to town on some business before and saw this kind of iron-plated cars. I have seen this car of yours too. Mr. Liu the deputy county chief always drove it around for a while. I only know that this kind of car runs fast, probably even faster than a deer, but I can't imagine a deer toppling a Bull Bear!"

I was baffled, unsure of the drift of the conversation, and looked beseechingly at Ah Rong for enlightenment.

Ah Rong seemed more at ease with Aqingbu than with Shuren. He was walking ahead of us; with three arrows held in his hand in a sheaf he was whipping away branches that threatened to get into his face, much like a mischievous child. He turned his head around and said in a teasing tone, "Don't you know? You are on the way to becoming a hero around here."

It turned out when the Bull Bear was carried back into the village, everyone was furious and vowed to disembowel me to avenge the "bear god." It was Shuren who temporarily shielded me from their wrath, but after a while when the villagers' initial outrage abated, some began to wonder: What kind of man could injure a god of their legend? How could the Bull Bear, of such massive build and commanding countless bears, according to legend, be so badly injured in the crash that it coughed up blood? And when they examined this captive of theirs—an ugly, cowardly, pale, corpulent fellow—he simply didn't seem to possess any physical strength.

Some nosy guys made special trips, across the mountains, to the crash site by the sheer cliff to examine that "iron-plated car"—a pile of metal like a crumpled cardboard box. When they kicked it, parts started falling off with a clang. That pile of junk looked in even worse shape than the fat guy who crashed it.

The car was totaled and the Bull Bear was incapacitated in the crash and yet the fat guy, miraculously, was unscathed and was still able to make daily sojourns, walking and running, along the periphery of the village, apparently full of energy. Everyone's attention was once again focused on the fat man. They privately speculated that this fat man must possess some special power. Some sought Shuren's opinion but Shuren only smiled to them, pointing to the half basket of wet firewood I had gathered. That prompted people to wonder if Shuren had kept something from them. If the fat man was only capable of gathering insignificant pieces of firewood, how could he have inflicted such grave injuries on the Bull Bear while remaining unhurt himself? If the fat man was indeed an effete, useless fellow, then were they to believe that the "bear god" mentioned with so much awe and reverence by generations of village elders was made of paper? This was a paradox Shuren was unprepared for.

For two months Shucun village was on the exterior as calm as the iced-over surface of a river in February, but down below a tiny crack had rapidly and imperceptibly developed into a huge cobweb of cracks visible only from below. If someone should take one step onto the frozen river, the ice extending to the horizon would open up with a huge roar and the foolhardy person would be swallowed by the rushing water of the river.

Therefore, Ah Rong was right, for in a sense I was indeed on the way to becoming a hero in the eyes of the Shucun villagers, certainly not because I seriously injured the Bull Bear but because what I did shook a millennial belief of the Shucun villagers to its foundation. I figured I was not unlike a Galileo who risked his life to challenge old thinking and bring enlightenment to the world, a kind of hero on the ideological plane.

I was basking in the new-found glory of being a hero when Aqingbu signaled with his big hand for me to stop in my tracks, a finger on his lips; then with a deft flip of his wrist he took the long bow from his shoulder. Before I could see it, the arrow was already let fly and disappeared in the trees. I was startled, wondering what just happened. I saw Ah Rong make a mark on a tree trunk with his small knife and put out his tongue while pointing at Aqingbu; then he lifted a finger as if counting. After ten paces, Ah Rong stopped to listen for two seconds with a cocked ear before swiftly arming his bow with an arrow and firing it off. He made another mark on the tree trunk and as he walked on he held high a finger triumphantly. Obviously he had scored one.

They appeared to be in a contest. It was only after Aqingbu had scored four and Ah Rong three that I, slow of hand and of eye as I was, found out they had shot rabbits. It turned out every time they stopped, it was because they had either sighted or heard the movements of a rabbit. Each lifting of the finger meant the killing of a rabbit with only one arrow. I saw a gray furry ball jerk around once or twice before lying still, and the tail of an arrow sticking straight up. They didn't bother to pick up their game. I figured they left marks on the tree trunks just so that they could retrieve them on their return.

Even in a hunt, and a contest at that, the two, true to their reputation as the number one and number two hunting experts of Shucun, were very laid back. Ah Rong kept up his bouncing gait ahead of us. Aqingbu actively engaged me in conversation, as if he could tell where his prey was without having to take his eyes away from me.

Aqingbu said that he had been longing for a chance to talk to me about certain things, which in the presence of Shuren he'd hesitated to bring up. I realized for the first time Aqingbu spoke fluent Han Chinese; he spoke with a good pronunciation and commanded a large vocabulary. Even Shuren couldn't speak as well he did. As village chief of Shucun, his daily business included attending regular meetings in the county town and reporting on the work of the village government. In other words, he was the most traveled of the Shucun villagers outside of the village.

He said he had seen electric lamps, which shone without having to be lit with kindling or a candle, and that if you didn't turn them off, they would stay lit. He had also seen an artisanal gun, about the length of a bow that could roar like a lion. The shot fired from it did not have a feathered tail like an arrow, but it could pierce a tree trunk whose girth was the circumference of a circle formed by two men linking their fully extended arms. He had also seen a phone through which someone on the other side of the mountains could, without raising his voice or shouting, sound as if he were right next to the other interlocutor this side of the mountains. Then there was the television, a small box in which people laughed or cried. He was told that those people were real people who lived in this world, although at the other end of the world, farther away than these mountains. He said that every time he came back with these stories, the villagers, while trusting him, refused to believe those fantastic things described by him, dismissing them as mere stories invented by him to amuse them.

At this point Aqingbu scratched his head; the tall bulky young man suddenly appeared a little bashful. "Fat One!" he said to me. "I know you don't have the knack for cutting wood and for hunting, but you know how to operate an iron-plated car. That's a powerful skill! Slogans plastered on walls in the county town in giant red characters read: science is power. You are probably the most powerful of the three of us."

I quickly waved my hands in self-deprecation, but I had a sense of walking on air.

Aqingbu continued, "Well, tell us about that science thing!" His copper-colored face was turned toward me in eager expectation; he exhibited a natural friendliness and his steady, unwavering look was heartening. Even his torso, with his mountain-like shoulders and big hands pressed upon his sinewy chest, appeared to testify to his sincerity.

Encouraged by the village chief's unexpected high opinion of me, my tongue ran away with me. How could someone who had spent a lot of time partying not be versed in the art of gab? Even though I was one of the clumsiest conversationalists at dinner tables in the urban setting, my gift of gab was certainly superior to the height of these mountains compared to the villagers. This was my first opportunity to demonstrate the superiority of a city person in Shucun village. Speech, which was only a tool for the Shucun villagers to express their thoughts, had uses that couldn't be further from its original intended purpose for city people.

I must have painted the world outside Shucun village into an extraterrestrial place, what with its high tech, market economy, international conflicts and the credit crisis. I knew Aqingbu was having a tough time wrapping his head around much of it, but he maintained a steady stride and his usual poise, occasionally interjecting a remark with a laugh. I was much impressed by this display of natural ease, which was part and parcel of his charisma as a leader. I therefore did my best to explain: "To sum it up, outside Shucun, people are the masters of the world. They build cities and reclaim land from the sea. They go into space and into the depths of the earth and the ocean. They slaughter animals and human populations, all in a day's work." Then I mentioned the original purpose of my business trip to Shucun: the satellite phone.

"But," I told Aqingbu, "in your present conditions, you have no need for it at all for the foreseeable future. The most practical thing for your village would be a hydro station and maybe a tractor, which will help improve basic living standards."

Aqingbu nodded thoughtfully.

Ah Rong was unable to join the conversation because of his unserviceable Han Chinese, but he was happy to have been the one to bring us together, a great achievement in his own estimation. He looked on as we walked abreast deep in conversation, now getting ahead of us, now falling behind and whistling in a low tone. All along the way as I talked without letup, their contest never missed a beat and they easily managed to kill another eight or nine rabbits each. Their total scores tied at thirteen. Because of the need to divide his attention between hunting and talking to me, Aqingbu was one rabbit behind Ah Rong.

At this time we emerged from the woods and came to a quiet clearing. In the bright sunshine rabbits, fawns, squirrels and larks went about their business, showing no fear of humans.

The three of us came to a stop. "Do you really believe that humans are the masters of the world?" Aqingbu suddenly asked me. "Every time I traveled to town, I saw mountains being blasted open, rivers being dammed up and the county town lit up at night; and people there butchered their pigs any time they liked. But in our village we've for generations lived at the mercy of the weather and the bears and we've been careful not to violate the taboos of our laws. We have bowed before all those powers. It is really degrading."

As we talked, a fawn approached us with its downy eyes blinking. It was barely a year old and the two antlers on its head were single spikes, not yet bifurcated, looking like two soft up-pointing braids of hair. Its fine hair, whose color was still a light shade of golden red, glistened in the sunlight as it moved, showing off its well-formed muscles. It stepped lightly and deftly like a ballet dancer. Its beauty, so close range, elicited an involuntary low cry of admiration from me.

Another deer came up to us. She was taller and could be the fawn's mother. The two deer rubbed against each other naturally as their paths crossed. The fawn playfully nudged the female deer's belly with its cheek.

Ah Rong and Aqingbu exchanged a glance and as if by previous agreement took down almost at the same moment the long bow from their shoulder and drew a feathered arrow out of their quiver. Ah Rong's arrow buried itself in the right hind leg of the fawn, while Aqingbu's went deep into the mother deer's right hind leg. The two deer instantly fell on their knees before struggling up and fleeing in fright with their injuries. Ah Rong and Aqingbu gave chase together, the tiny animal tusks ornamenting their braided hair tinkling in their motion and brushing across my face.

The deer, even with an injured hind leg, still ran fast. The hunters' gallop looked deceptively like a walk, and I had to break into a run to catch up with them. The trail of blood on the grass was a shock to my eyes. The fawn was the first to slow down, then the mother deer slackened her pace, loath to abandon the fawn it seemed. There was a flash before my eyes and two more arrows pierced the air to land respectively in the left hind leg of the fawn and the mother deer. It had the look of an amusing game, for all I knew.

The two deer continued their desperate flight, only at a much slower speed. Ah Rong and Aqingbu exchanged another glance and smile and continued their pursuit with supreme confidence; they could have been playing an eighteen-hole game of golf. After a distance, arrows left their bows again. Every time the two hunters shot their arrow into the same spot on the body of either deer, never fatally—left rump, right rump, right foreleg, left foreleg.

The thought of congratulating the two hunters on their brilliant feat of archery had now left me. I stumbled along the blood-splattered path, dizzied and nauseated by the sight of the suffering of the two deer. Somehow I suddenly recalled the inner demons mentioned by Shuren. Were the man full of fervor and resolve and the friendly, sprightly boy who had walked all the way up the mountains with me the same two guys who now derived such great thrills from using a young fawn as their live target for practice?

I saw the elation in their face. As time went by their pace slowed as their stride took on greater authority. The two deer were now no better than two writhing hedgehogs on the ground. I couldn't decide if I should follow them or turn around and steal away from them. An enormous fear rose in me, a hollow kind of fear that kept expanding. I felt that my world was swept into a maelstrom of nightmarish emptiness. I opened my mouth to scream but no sound came out. I tried to struggle free but I couldn't wipe that ingratiating smile off my face. It was a fear that was at once extremely familiar and yet far removed from the here and now. It occurred to me that this eerie feeling had gripped me more than on one occasion: in front of the tightly shut door of the office of vice president Carl, in the noxious odor of strawberry vodka mixed with roast fish, at the moment William shoved Mary into the lap of Old John and when Jessica fiddled with the platinum Guanyin pendant with her beautiful fingers.

Somehow I felt that it could very well be me in the place of the deer riddled with arrows rolling and writhing on the ground, while others looked on with a triumphant smile.

The game of golf with deer as trophy continued. The deer received twelve arrows each and finally collapsed and gave up their struggle, looking with glazed eyes at the approaching hunters. Aqingbu took a step back and with an avuncular smile deferred to Ah Rong, signaling him to administer the coup de grace with one last arrow. With a resplendent smile Ah Rong took aim at the head of the fawn. As he drew the bow into a full moon the mother deer made one last jerking motion to shield the fawn and received the arrow in her belly.

The aroma of barbecued deer meat was hard to resist; the birds and squirrels had scattered. Only the two hind legs of the fawn were cooked over the fire because the three of us would not be able to finish two deer in one meal. I did not have any appetite for the barbecued meat at first, but Aqingbu said with a laugh: "When the meat is done, your appetite will come back." And he was right. The aroma tempted me, and hunger from the long hike through the mountains nudged me toward the venison. I accepted a piece of a hind leg from Ah Rong's hand and fell to with gusto. It was tender and juicy and pleasured my mouth.

Aqingbu also cut off a slice of deer meat with the dagger he carried on him and handed it to me: "Fat One! You know the meat tastes best when the deer is less than a year old. Once a deer is past the age of one, it will no longer taste this good. If you hadn't come with us, you'd probably never have taken a bite of this delicacy."

I mumbled a perfunctory reply, concentrating on the food and thinking to myself: What's so special about this? The milling masses of city people have always eaten chickens less than a year old, except when they make chicken soup, which calls for tougher, older birds.

My teeth came in contact with something hard; it was not the bone. After I finished off the meat, I examined the bone and found a copper arrowhead embedded in it. They had pulled out all the arrows when the legs were prepared for the barbecue, but a few penetrated deep into the bone. This was left by the arrow shot by Ah Rong into the fawn's right hind leg. When Aqingbu tried to pull it out, his face became crimson with the effort and he blurted out a good-humored backhanded compliment: "Hey, you shoot better than ever!" Finally the arrow had to be cut out with a knife and the meat was roasted with the arrowhead left in.

All of a sudden my stomach turned violently and I nearly threw up all the food I had just ingested. I felt deeply ashamed of my robust appetite.

The fire died down. Next to the charred grass stood the two soft antlers of the fawn; only the upper half of its beautiful golden red body remained. Its eyes had begun to turn murky, staring fixedly into the blue sky with a blazing sun. The mother deer lay next to it, its body covered with blood and its lips slightly parted.

I had thought they would bag their game. But it was heavy. How could the two manage to carry it back? What would they say when they returned with the trophy? Would they say they'd hunted despite the prohibitions of the laws? Apparently they had thought about the matter ahead of time and left behind the two carcasses. At each marked tree, they retrieved the arrow from the rabbit shot by either of them and left the rabbit behind. The arrows would be needed for the next hunting expedition. By my count, out of the twenty-six arrows in each of their quivers, thirteen were used to kill rabbits, and the other thirteen were shot into the deer. The two hunters, taking great pride in their skills, had pointedly taken with them only the exact number of arrows they needed. This obviously was not the first time they'd played this kind of hunting games despite the prohibitions of the laws.

I once asked Shuren why he had declared humans to be too tainted—far less pure than animals—and unfit to be sacrificed to the gods. Did he say that in front of the murderous crowd only to save me from being slaughtered or did he have a basis for saying so?

"Of course humans are the dirtiest," Shuren replied. "When an animal kills another animal, it always does so for a legitimate reason: it needs food to sustain its life. After finishing off its kill, it will not again hurt another animal gratuitously before the next hunger pangs. Humans are different. Humans hunt and toy with their victims out of some mysterious psychological need. They relish the sport and never tire of it. Prejudice and cruelty are unique to humans."

With an unsteady tread I followed Aqingbu and Ah Rong. On our return the fear in me never left me in peace for a minute. I was frightened of them and even more of myself—the delectable taste of the tender venison still clung to my palate. When either of them spoke to me, they would find me staring and blinking as if I were startled out of a dream. My heart would be pounding hard. They attributed it to my fatigue and left me in peace.

We were approaching the five clusters of houses. All of a sudden we were struck by panic when we saw Shuren waiting in the main road cutting across the plain. The illegal hunt must have been found out! Like a group of criminals filing meekly into a prison cage, we walked with a faltering step, wishing we could just throw away our bows and arrows, burn them to ashes and make them disappear.

"You come with me," Shuren said, and then glanced at Aqingbu, "you too." He did not ask Ah Rong to follow him.

At the door of the big house a tall and corpulent figure was pacing impatiently about. At the sight of me, he immediately threw away the half-smoked Double Happiness cigarette in his hand and waddled toward me at a brisk pace. "My eldest son, I've finally found you!" he cried, clasping me in his arms.

I asked Liu Yushan expectantly who was looking for me.

With a sharp look at me, Deputy County Chief Liu said, "Who else?"

Two months after I drove out of the county town, Liu Yushan started missing his best car one day; then it occurred to him all of a sudden that he had not had the presence of mind to give me enough gasoline to enable me to make the trip back to the county town. As for me, I hadn't the faintest idea who I was expecting to come looking for me.

On this second meeting with me, Liu Yushan had promoted me straight to "my eldest son" from the previous "my young cousin." Aqingbu said, with sudden understanding, looking me up and down: "I should have guessed. You look so much alike! No wonder you drove his car and share the last name Liu!"

X

I didn't immediately leave with Liu Yushan, even though in the long months before his visit not one day went by without me wishing wholeheartedly to break out of this prison.

It appeared that this place that imprisoned me had subtly grown on me. Besides, I still had to resolve the matter for which I bore responsibility. I asked Lu Yushan to send someone on my behalf to the animal hospital in Kunming and buy a few cases of etamsylate, some vitamin K2 and cephradine. Doing some math based on the body weight of the Bull Bear, I decided that the oral dosage for it would be a hundred fold higher than for small dogs. The herbal concoctions had not produced significant benefit. If this situation was allowed to drag on, I was afraid the Bull Bear could very well spend the rest of its life lying prostrate in the big house, unable to ever be on its feet again.

"So there is indeed a Bull Bear!" It had become a repeated refrain from Liu Yushan's lips. He had told the story countless times; now he finally got to meet the protagonist of the story. He circled the hemp mat a few times with a soft tread, bending down to have a close look, uttering a string of tsk-tsk-tsk of admiration. "What a splendid piece of pelt this would make!" he blurted out. Then, suddenly sensing the disapproving looks from the people around him, he quickly shut up.

"It was thanks to it that I have not become a pile of bleached bones at the foot of a cliff," I said.

Deputy County Chief Liu lit another Double Happiness cigarette and crouched down on a large rock in front of the house. Looking askance at me he asked with a half laugh: "Tell me, did the bear come into the road to deliberately block your passage or did you crash into it by accident? It seems to me you've stayed too long in this god-forsaken place and it is making you dumb and a little daft."

The Bull Bear was getting better by the day, this time without any relapses. This was attributable to its cooperation in swallowing those pills, or more accurately, chewing and not swallowing those pills. The expression on its face when the medicine finally went down its throat caused my pharynx to tighten as if I were swallowing a bitter pill myself.

When one day it finally got to its feet and walked slowly back into the forest, there was a tingle in my nose as I watched its sluggish bulk recede into the distance and become a reddish brown shimmer. I felt sad because I was departing too, leaving this serene Shangri-La and the elderly Shuren who had been so kind to me.

Shuren appeared to have read my mind; he said in a soft tone: "Son, we will meet again."

"Well, not very likely," I said.

Shuren was very sure. "We will meet again. I know."

I was back in the office building on Huaihai Road, took the elevator up, met colleagues, whose spring suits had by now given way to summer dresses. They nodded greetings to me in the usual manner, as if I had said good night to them only yesterday at the door of the elevator at six in the afternoon. I was confused; could it be that my months-long stay at Shucun had been merely a strange dream I had just before dawn in my half-awake state?

In uneasy confusion I pressed the button for Jessica's floor. I had an urgent need to see a most familiar face before riding up to my office. Jessica was more beautiful than in early spring; her hair had been redesigned, now with curls of it tied behind her ears. She wore an ivory white, body-fitting suit that set off her trim figure; her skin had a rosy tint and her eyelashes were dark and long. She spotted me through the glass door and a smile flickered across her face, like a flitting butterfly. She was very busy.

I went in. She lifted her face. "Hey, you're back. Is everything fine? I see that you've acquired a tan," she greeted me as if I had just come back from a vacation.

With her fingers dancing all over the keyboard, she answered two urgent emails before turning her head around. "I already knew yesterday that you were back. Well, have you rested up?"

I was at a loss to answer these cordial inquiries. I was rooted there, my tongue tied; I didn't even know if I should sit down. I had expected a look of startled joy, tears, tremors in the voice and a warm embrace. Or a severe scolding for my ominous disappearance: "Hey, you swine! I was worried to death for your sake!" What went wrong, I wondered. Had my understanding of humans become so outdated after two months spent in bear country?

Carl happened to drop in at this time. He held out his hand when he was still some distance from me and said with a booming voice and a laugh: "Old pal! Sorry to trouble you to come in!" His smile was contagious and the offer of a handshake was cordial, but no sooner had his palm come in contact with my fingers— just a brief brush—than his hand was withdrawn before I could grasp it.

He said: "Old pal, as you know, the donation of the satellite phone has dragged on for so long now and the matter of government procurement has been held up. That's why you have been called in the day after your return to attend an emergency meeting. Sorry to trouble you to come in! Just wait. When this thing comes to fruition, I will tell personnel to grant you a special leave of a few days! After your long disappearance, it pains me to give you more days off, ha-ha-ha." After this peal of laughter, Carl placed a stack of documents on the desk of Jessica, who immediately proceeded to go through them as Carl gave instructions to her.

Jessica suddenly looked up with a smile and said to me in a rushed tone, "Give your best at the meeting!"

That was the cue for me to leave. I took the elevator to the floor of the marketing department and walked past rows of cubicles. My eyes, of their own accord, strayed to where Mary sat. She was poring over documents. I was sure she knew I was approaching, but she remained stubbornly still, keeping her head down. I had no cause for complaint. It's not as if I'd ever been of much help to her. Merely to feel good about myself, I had put her vulnerability as a single mother to further risk and it was she who ended up paying for my vanity. I had no doubt that during my disappearance her life must have been made more miserable because of my indiscreet intervention.

William and Thomas were probably the most delighted to see me back. As head of the department that sent me on the ill-fated business trip, William could not expect to shirk blame for the incident and he had to explain himself by filing multiple reports. It was said that Thomas was disciplined for not having found out my whereabouts with due diligence, thus taking part of the blame for William.

Thomas placed his hands on my shoulders and, with a contrived air of sophistication, lowered his gaze at me, like an adult looking at a child. He sighed and said, deadpan: "Boss, I was worried to death about you!" Once again I was almost touched by the apparent sincerity on his face, only inches away.

William asked me about the circumstances of my disappearance so that he could write a final report summarizing all previous ones. All I said was I had a car accident in an isolated location, broke a bone and not being able to contact anybody was compelled to stay there to recover from my injuries. I didn't know what got into me. On my way back from the wilderness, I couldn't wait to share my fantastic experience in Shucun village with people I knew, but the moment I was among a human crowd, I suddenly felt a great reluctance to say anything to them, particularly to those smiling faces in my office.

At the emergency meeting to discuss the gift of a satellite phone, William and Old John were both very quiet.

Old John kept adjusting the silk scarf inside his shirt collar. The meeting was chaired by Carl. At the close of the opening presentation of basic facts, he said as a formality: "I invite the president to comment first." It took several promptings before Old John stopped deferring to others and said in his low voice and an inflective tone: "High management can't be expected to attend to every detail. This is routine work of the marketing department and a matter that can be handled within the marketing department. I don't believe there's a need to call a meeting of the entire middle- and high-level management staff."

After making those remarks, Old John sipped his tea imperturbably, with downcast eyes and as urbane as ever. Carl maintained his celebrity smile, giving the impression that Old John had said something inspirational. He led the meeting in applause before resuming, without missing a beat, his pep talk.

William's eyes and finger never left the screen of his smartphone and to every question raised by Carl, he responded with an earnest smile and ah's, oh's, eh's and yes-yes-yes.

Carl spoke of China Mobile's contract tender for the provinces of Jiangxi, Sichuan, Fujian and Yunnan worth about 800 million yuan, the aggressive moves of the rival SME and the superhuman efforts made by Jessica's team in the sales department and the enormous difficulties they faced; he also presented a vision of HZ Communications China's entry in the world's electronic communications industry's who's who once it was able to make a successful bid for the contract.

After the *tour d'horizon*, he once again stressed the importance of building an alliance with Yunnan Mobile and the donation of a satellite phone to its impoverished areas. At this point his eyes rested approvingly on my face for a few seconds. It was apparent that the name of Shucun village temporarily eluded him. He said that society's perception of a corporation was pivotal in modern corporate competition. Sometimes a winning strategy was more effective than a company's real strength in deciding the outcome of the competition.

All through his speech, Jessica followed him with a rapt eye and ear, frequently nodding and jotting down notes. Jessica was only now turning her eyes toward me.

Carl was now summing up. "This gift of a satellite phone needs immediate execution. It brooks no delay! Kevin, are you confident you can accomplish this in the shortest order?"

"Frankly," I said, "Shucun village doesn't need a satellite phone."

A startled look leapt into Jessica's eyes.

Carl's smile froze.

Old John accidentally dropped the lid of his teacup, producing a sharp clink against it.

There was the incongruous sound of someone beating time: it was William, the toes of whose Ermenegildo Zegna shoes were smugly tapping a chair. He stopped the rapping, nonchalantly looked left and right at the hushed audience, shook his shoulder-length long hair back and sat up.

"Why are you doing this? Why? Are you brain-dead?"

Jessica chided me in a suppressed voice, firing off her words as if from a machine gun, and stared angrily at me with her big eyes opened to the size of apricots. As her delicate manicured hands fidgeted on the table, I had a distinct fear that she might grab the cup of hot cappuccino in anger and dump the content on my face.

Luckily the second floor of the Starbucks in the Xintiandi mall was not crowded that afternoon. We would otherwise have made such a public spectacle of ourselves in public, even if the other patrons couldn't make out what she was saying.

"Do you," she said, "do you know, Kevin, that with that casual little sentence of yours you destroyed in one stroke this golden opportunity that so many of us have been waiting and working for all these years?"

The delivery of this rather long statement lost none of its

gale-force momentum for all the pauses for breath and the bitterness gathered strength with each additional word spewed out of her mouth. She spread her hands, joined them, and spread them anew, as if trying to add emphasis to the accusatory tone. I noticed that her French tip nails were kept longer than before and trimmed to a new almond shape, with a lily applique on every tip. Clawing the air, she was the picture of a provoked cat.

I believed her anxiety was uncalled for. She shouldn't be such a workaholic, and there was no reason why she should be so hung up about the matter. She was already a branch manager in this foreign-capital enterprise. For a female employee and a Chinese national, this was the top; she had hit the glass ceiling. She could see higher positions through that glass, but she wouldn't be able to rise to that level, no matter how outstanding her performance. This is a rule in foreign-capital enterprises in China. In other words, she had "arrived," with job security and a high salary. There was no reason for her to get so worked up.

Her chest heaving and her pretty face becoming red and white by turns, she enumerated on her fingers the various ways in which I had "undermined" the grand battle for the prized contract.

Old John, the President, had behind him a coterie of company "moderates." For Old John himself, all he needed to do was stick with HZ Communications China until retirement without making any major mistakes, when he would receive his pension benefits comparable to the standards of the HZ Asia-Pacific Headquarters and cash in the stock options promised him. He would also get to return to the HZ corporate headquarters as a member on the board of the parent company.

As for those that followed him, such as the likes of William, once Old John was on the board of the HZ corporate headquarters, he would naturally have an opportunity to recommend their transfer to the company headquarters, which would be tantamount to putting them on the fast track to career advancement in the industry.

But Old John was four years away from retirement; not everyone could wait that long.

There was another faction in the company, the "radicals," led by Vice President Carl, whose succession to the position of president was a foregone conclusion. The possibility of further movement, say, a transfer to the high management of the HZ headquarters was not so certain. Carl was 43; as a rule headquarters would basically not consider anyone past 45 for grooming or promotion. By the time Old John retired as planned, Carl would be over that age threshold and live out his career in the present company. This scenario was certainly unacceptable to Carl.

Therefore Old John must go before then. This was to be accomplished either by finding major mistakes made by Old John, or by Carl's aggressive pursuit of high, spectacular performance in order to show Old John up as the feckless president he was.

Carl's faction had racked their brains and worked at it for four years now and Jessica joined their scheming three years ago when she joined HZ from another company. Old John was careful not to provide ammunition to the other faction, and his position gave him greater powers. Besides, his was not exactly a faction of gentlemanly types. The factional fight was long drawn-out and only two years separated them from that fateful threshold date. Suddenly a perfect opportunity presented itself in the form of a government procurement project worth nearly 800 million yuan, and sales happened to be a strong suit of Carl and Jessica. If they succeeded in landing the contract, it would be a direct slap in the face of Old John, a slap so crisp the entire industry would hear it. A resounding success was the hope of many, until a trouble maker suddenly dampened that hope—I naturally was that trouble maker.

I would readily admit that I was that proverbial ant responsible for the failure of a thousand-mile dike. But Jessica insisted that I ruined "so many people," that I trifled with their lives. Was office infighting as bad as that?

Jessica kept twirling the pendant on her necklace. It was

that same platinum Guanyin pendant. I had always been puzzled by the fact that Jessica, who had European tastes, listened to symphonies, played the piano, loved oil paintings, read foreign novels in translation, wore western formal dresses and never a *qi pao* (cheongsam), had picked a pendant like that. She bit her lips and fiddled obsessively with the pendant, oblivious to the fact that her nails had scratched a red line across the skin below her neck. A few seconds later, I saw tears streaking down her cheeks as she started to sob; she picked up two paper napkins from the table. I went to the sugar and napkins stand to fetch a whole stack of napkins for her.

She said: "I've been branch manager for seven long years, seven years! I've hopped from company to company in hopes of moving to a higher position to no avail. You don't know how I want to move up. It's what I think about twenty-four hours a day. I'd give an eye for it! Why did you do this to me?"

"Carl promised if we succeed in driving Old John out before his retirement time, he will definitely promote me to vice president of HZ Communications China," she said. "If an opportunity comes up for an even higher position, he will help me get it. Why should I be a perpetual branch manager? Why should I forever be at the beck and call of high management? Why is my name destined to be kept out of the who's who of the electronic communications industry?"

"It is possible that HZ Communications China will expand in a few years and see its ranking in the industry rise. If I am promoted to vice president, then I will have an opportunity to become president, and I will be in the who's who and a part of the history of the industry, and will receive invitations to all high-level meetings and conventions of the industry ..." She glared at me with teary eyes: "Do you realize what you just did to me?"

Jessica took down her necklace and opened the platinum Guanyin pendant with her fingernail. In the little box with a hinged lid was a black paper sack of a hexagonal shape. When she took it out of the case, it immediately opened like a butterfly to stand on the coffee table; on it was a string of characters in red ink that didn't make any sense to me. Those strange characters looked not unlike the incantations drawn by Shuren with cinnabar. I suddenly understood what it was.

It was a very odd feeling; I tried very hard to stifle the hilarity exploding inside of me over the fact that this office lady in a prime office building in the cosmopolitan city of Shanghai should place such pious hopes in mysterious powers allegedly originating from primitive society! Her thirst for career advancement must have reached a fever pitch. Even as my guts were tied up in knots with hilarity, I was filled with an indescribable horror at what I witnessed.

Fixing me with a dreadful stare Jessica said with swollen eyes: "I asked a friend to obtain this incantation for me from Yunnan last year. It is very powerful; it can guarantee my career advancement and no mean-spirited man will succeed in stopping me from climbing up the corporate ladder."

The mention of a "mean-spirited man" was naturally an oblique swipe at me. I asked sheepishly: "How is Carl?"

Jessica said: "He is mad of course! In fact he is so mad he doesn't want to see your face at the moment. It was very indecent of you to have said what you said. You should be ashamed of yourself."

My crime was bad enough to cause Carl the executive with a permanent celebrity smile to lose his temper and the workaholic Jessica to abandon her department during office hours and drag me to the Xintiandi mall to berate me in tears.

It was indeed indecent of me. On the eve of leaving for Shucun village, I defected to them for Mary's sake. They were totally convinced of my allegiance to their camp. That was why Carl didn't feel a need to coach me before the meeting. He had total trust in me doing the right thing. He was unprepared for my betrayal at the last moment.

After her bout of crying, which left the table covered with used napkins and her eyelids swollen, Jessica regained her usual clear, calm thinking. "Kevin, you must be trying to maintain neutrality," she said to me. "Let me tell you, in the office you'll never be able to keep neutral. If you insist on doing it, the only result is you'll be regarded as an odd man out and you'll be trampled under their feet, insulted, ridiculed and bullied. Do you really think you can stand being stuck at the bottom rungs? When you are stuck there you won't find an idyllic life; instead, you'll end up with emotional problems if not financial ones also."

"Jessica, please give me a chance to speak. Neutrality or not, the fact is Shucun village does not need a satellite phone. I stayed there for two months and I should know. They have absolutely no need to communicate with the outside world. They don't even know what a phone is. If we really want to help the poor and needy, why not give them a few bullocks for tilling, or a tractor?"

Blinking her eyes, Jessica said: "Kevin, have you been brainwashed by the savages during your two months spent there?"

I knew what she meant: whether the publicity campaign would go forward was driven not by the needs of the intended recipients of the gift but by the needs of one or the other faction in the office. I thought bitterly: what kind of business is this that makes pawns of villagers in a remote, impoverished area?

Without my noticing it, Jessica was observing my facial expression. Suddenly she had a revelation and a bitter look of having been fooled crept into her face. With a stern expression she asked: "Kevin, you are playing dumb with me, right? Have you switched fealty to the camp of Old John and William? Are you doing their bidding? Are you sitting here secretly gloating over our misfortune?"

There was a steely glint in her eyes as she watched me.

William organized a dinner to honor my homecoming and made sure Mary was seated next to me. That evening they made Mary drink cup after cup with me, with our cup-holding arms crossed and intertwined. Mary averted her eyes all the while, with not a ghost of a smile on her pale face, and with her shoulders hunched and her head bowed pensively when she was not called on to do something.

Thomas also drank countless toasts to me, as if he was conspiring with William to drink me under the table. What with the rest of the crowd scrambling to follow suit, my consciousness soon blurred. They ordered me to finish the entire plate of roasted fish as punishment, saying I had made them wait too long for my return and that I needed nourishment after having been in exile in the wild for so long. I had to lick the entire dish clean, greasy sauce and all.

I was sick in the bathroom for a long time. When I returned, I saw William greeting me with a raised glass. Shaking his long hair, he rose to his feet and said: "Attention please! This dinner is in honor of Kevin, who just ended his Robinson Crusoe days and returned to the civilized world blessed with telephones and to our marketing department." His words were greeted with an uproar of laughs and a round of clapping.

Holding out his other hand, with the palm down, he signaled silence before continuing: "We've hosted two welcome dinners in honor of Kevin in six months. That means Kevin is a very popular guy. You find only merits in him: he protects women, he has outstanding survival skills, he has an honest nature, he never lies and he puts justice above everything. He has only one shortcoming."

At this point William put a hand over his chest and turned to me with a commiserating expression on his face: "Your only shortcoming is you pay too little attention to protecting yourself! You belong not only to yourself, but are also an asset of the marketing department. How could you so carelessly allow yourself to suffer a fracture? In order to make everyone aware of the importance of self-protection and to draw a lesson from your experience, I am demoting you as of today. From now on Thomas will be your supervisor."

XI

I began to strive for an idyllic life at HZ Communications, in other words, a life of contentment at the bottom. I punctually punched in and out every day, worked diligently, tried my best not to make any mistake that could be used against me and waited for periodic salary raises. I thought to myself: this is the worst scenario and I can handle it.

Since becoming my boss, Thomas quite enjoyed talking to me. He must be getting a great sense of fulfilment from having someone ten years his senior at his beck and call. He also tried to be patronizingly bonhomous with me. It was uncommon for someone as young as he to understand the need to be affable and accessible.

One day at noon he gave me a stack of documents about three feet high to copy and staple. Toward the end of the working day, probably to assuage his conscience, he sauntered over to the copier and started a chat, with one hand on the wall and the other in his pocket. He asked me: "Old pal, is your leg still hurting these days?" Since becoming my boss, he took to mimicking Carl's tone when speaking to me, even though he was only a low-level supervisor.

I shot back: "My leg is not hurting. It's my back that's hurting now. As you can see, I've already bent several thousand times over this machine this afternoon."

The scanning light of the copier swept across his face. I lifted the lid, removed the page and bent down to take the next page from the pile to feed into the copier. I heard him say, in an eager tone: "Hey, tell me about Shucun village, just to pass the time."

I replied without enthusiasm: "It's so impoverished it's not served by any highway. To eat flat bread, they have to plant their own wheat. To eat meat, they have to hunt for rabbits. They even have to weave their own fabrics in order to clothe themselves. So what's there to tell?"

Very casually he picked up what I just said. "Then tell me why you stayed so long there and nearly thought about not coming back."

All of a sudden I glimpsed the hidden daggers in this conversation he was steering. So I also replied with feigned casualness: "The truth is I didn't have a fractured leg. I was caught up in something much more serious than that. Old pal, I'm saying this only to you. You mustn't disclose it to anyone."

And I truthfully related the whole story, lock, stock and barrel, to Thomas: how the car I was driving crashed into the bear god, how I was carried on a pole by hunters into Shucun Village and became a captive, how I was nearly slaughtered as sacrifice to the Bull Bear and was saved from that dire fate only by the intervention of the Elder and how I suddenly was transformed into a Galileo-like figure and treated by the village chief as an honored guest. I drew the story out, temporizing; every time I bent over the stack of documents, I deliberately interjected a long pause in my story-telling. Soon Thomas started bending down to pick up the next sheet for me to copy. The parking lot below seen through the glass wall was emptying out as cars left until the last car drove away at dusk. Thomas kept his patience and waited to catch the next line of my story. I did not intend to have this helper leave my side before the copying and collating of all the documents were completed.

That Thomas was a smart, hard-working spy was obvious. My story was exactly the intelligence he had yearned to gather.

I knew it was time to get rid of me once and for all and all

William was waiting for was a reason, such as the fact that in the incident of my disappearance, for which William and Thomas had been severely criticized, I in fact did not suffer a fracture and had neglected my duty and gone AWOL for two and a half months.

Two days later the intelligence I fed Thomas had an immediate effect. After work, the whole department left with William for a dinner party, leaving just me and Thomas in the office. Without deigning to look at me, he packed up his briefcase in a huff, turned on his heels and left by the stairs.

There is said to be a technique in spy craft called reverse intelligence. I did not provide any false information to Thomas; everything I told him was absolutely true, except that no city people, with the exception of Thomas, who couldn't wait to claim credit in front of William, would believe an outlandish story and experience like mine. I could perfectly imagine how, after having hearing Thomas out, William would say: "Hey, brother! Isn't this invented story a little too farfetched? Are you trying to do him in or help him do me in?"

If a spy provides unreliable information just once, all future information gathered by him will be discredited. Under the circumstances, that was the most I was able to accomplish.

But when you are given a manifest destiny, there's no escaping it.

The long summer came to an end. One day, HZ Communications received a letter from the Organization Department of the government of Xuyang County of Yunnan Province, in which it thanked HZ Communications for its support of their development efforts and made a special mention of my name.

"We are grateful to comrade Liu Kai for his selfless dedication to the welfare of the people of Shucun village. His work there has earned the heartfelt gratitude of the villagers. Shucun village, a remote and impoverished part of our county, has for years been plagued by a severe shortage of means of transport and communications. Since comrade Liu Kai's departure, Shucun village has sent representatives to the county government on several occasions to voice the hope that comrade Liu Kai would consent to return to Shucun to continue what he has started there and to set up the satellite phone at an early date. Shucun village is very unique in culture and customs and it was no mean feat for an outsider to have been able to work with the villagers. The county party committee and county government wish to warmly welcome comrade Liu Kai back to pick up where he left off as soon as possible and promise full support and cooperation."

XII

So I was back to Shucun village.

This time the car was driven by a chauffeur of the county government and Liu Yushan accompanied me on the trip. Aqingbu and Ah Rong met us at the end of the highway and led us through that only access road to the plain. I was out of breath the entire way and I often needed to be supported, helped and dragged along as I was not steady of foot. And I requested frequent rest stops. As a result the trek took the best part of six hours.

Aqingbu wasn't bothered at all by the slow progress of the walking party; he kept up a spirited conversation with me. He said that gossip had not died down with my departure. On the contrary since it was I and not Shuren who healed the Bull Bear, Shuren's status as an icon among the villagers suffered a big setback. Some even floated the idea of making me a successor to the Elder, for the Elder's other function was as the only doctor in the village, be he called a practitioner of traditional medicine or a witch doctor, on whom the villagers depended for the treatment of all injuries and illnesses. He was said to possess an "azure power" to relieve disease and pain, vested in him by the sky. But it seemed that the sky was no longer looking with favor upon Shuren but had instead manifested its magic powers through me.

It was a great shock to me. I had never meant any harm to Shuren or wanted to see the kindness and authority of this elderly man questioned. I tried to explain to Aqingbu and Ah Rong that it was only a very common drug that any city person could easily get at an animal clinic, that it was no magic power on my part. I pulled Liu Yushan toward us and asked him to corroborate what I said, but he only smiled, without saying a word.

With a twitch of his mouth Aqingbu seemed to indicate he didn't care if I possessed magic powers or not and he was in no hurry to find out what kind of science made possible the recovery of the Bull Bear.

He said to me: "Fat One, all I know is you are a friend, a good friend!" He dragged me up a steep slope littered with fallen rocks, almost lifting me off the ground. He said: "You suffered so much, just so you could help bring progress to this village. Everybody now understands this. They want to see what life will be like for them when progress really comes to us."

I didn't know what to say in answer; maybe I did the right thing by coming back here after all.

Finally the familiar beautiful plain in the shape of five petals came into sight.

But as I reached the periphery of the plain I was greeted by an astonishing sight. At the entrance of the village stood a stone stele facing the trail that led into the mountains. Did someone die in the village during my short absence of a few months? A carousel of familiar, serene faces flashed through my mind. When Aqingbu realized we were all staring at the stele, an abashed look suddenly came into his face. Rubbing his cheeks with his outsized hands, he said with a blush: "It is for my son."

Ah Rong hastened to explain: "He erected this stele here after an incident in which his son suffered a fright."

He did what he could to translate the words written in a local language consisting of strokes and hooks. It went something like: "May the string of the bow snap when it is drawn back and may all arrows be deflected by this stele! Pray passers-by each recite this once, to restore peace and calm and bring rapid recovery to my beloved son!"

It was common knowledge that Aqingbu's wife was the most beautiful woman under the roofs of the five settlements of houses. She was proficient in dying, weaving and salting meats, but had produced only one son, Mila, for Aqingbu. Mila, who was seven at this time, had a weak constitution and fragile health. Despite a bulky frame, his walk was unsteady and he was racked by coughing seven months out of the year. As a consequence he had a completely different set of nerves than Aqingbu and his lips often tended to be pressed tightly together out of nervosity and his eyes were clouded by melancholy and unease.

Aqingbu sired this son much like a blazing sun giving birth to a thin sliver of dim new moon. Aqingbu and his wife adored this only son. But the fact remained that this kid always brought up the rear among his peers in learning hunting skills. The most egregious example of this was an incident in which he hesitated in front of a rabbit with his bow fully drawn and in the end he eased it back. That was a blow to the dignity and honor of Aqingbu, the number one hunter of Shucun village.

In the season of my absence from Shucun village, a marvelous change occurred in the forests; it was the season of annual courtship among the "bears with a human face." There were marriages and births among them. Furry bear cubs too many to enumerate appeared all over the place on the plain, romping around mother bears like so many fuzzballs. The fuzzballs rapidly grew in size; they toddled and tripped often, like awkward, timid kids.

For all that bears and humans coexisted peacefully and in good will for the other nine months of the year, in these three months, mother bears with cubs in tow pointedly avoided humans. The behavior, unchanging for years, was motivated by overanxious maternal love. But Mila had been seen playing often with two bear cubs by the river, while the mother bear stood watching at a distance. Maybe Mila appeared to her to be too frail, or maybe the look in his eyes held more kindness and gentleness than bears.

An unfortunate accident inevitably occurred. It was a blazing hot afternoon. Mila and the bear cubs were feeling for the ice cold backs of small fish in the golden river, when Mila slipped and instinctively reached out to grab a cub to keep his balance. Suddenly he felt himself thrown down by a powerful force and was gasping for breath. In a blur of dark shadows hovering over him, he sensed that his body was falling backwards with a splash into the river, sending up an explosion of spume. The water felt burning and excruciatingly painful on his shoulders.

On the shoulder of the child the mother bear left three deep claw marks. That was not all, he suffered a great fright. Shuren came several times to treat him; after the application of a poultice over the wound, it soon formed scabs and healed, leaving a desiccated scar raised high above the skin. But then the kid started refusing to get out of bed, lying in a state of torpor all day, his small eyes filled with terror and confusion. A door swinging in a breeze, a bird flying past the window or someone's footsteps outside the brick wall would trigger a terrified bout of crying. Even the familiar caresses of his father and mother would cause great anxiety in him. Curling himself into a fetal position, he sweated profusely and raved deliriously.

Shuren performed an exorcism on him. Afterwards he said shaking his head: "The kid has a heart of gold. There's no evil spirit in him at all. If he had never seen bow and arrow, he would probably not have been frightened by a bear."

I still lived in Shuren's big house this time around. Shuren still examined me with all the soft wrinkles on his face screwed up, surveying me from head to toe, touching my arms, patting my belly and brushing aside the sweat-drenched locks of hair falling over my forehead; then he would smile admiringly with a gentle shake of his head, like an elderly father pleased by the sight of a long absent son in good health and robust of body. It was as if the restiveness among the villagers mentioned by Aqingbu had never happened.

Shucun village maintained a surface calm.

Every day at dusk the familiar chorus of thanksgiving chants still rang out across the plain: *jia-luo-ni-jia-yeh, mo-lo-mo-lo*; like music, it salved my wrinkled heart. When the sun sank behind the mountain ridges, groups of worried parents would come calling on Shuren. Sitting in front of him and holding his heavily wrinkled hands, they all asked similar questions: "Will the bears hurt my children too? If they do, and we are forbidden to use force against them, what will happen to the children?"

Shuren heaved a discreet sigh when the visitors were not likely to notice. He smiled to these nervous parents and said with certainty in his tone: "Bears bear no ill will. If you believe the bears will not hurt your children, then they won't."

This reassurance failed to smooth the deep furrows on the parents' brows. To a large degree, their trust in the bears derived from their trust in Shuren, and in their trust they didn't bother to savor the deeper meaning behind these words. Shuren did not give a promise; he merely pointed out an important fact, i.e. malice exists only in one's mind. What one fears is often the mirror image of one's inner thought.

Before leaving, the parents tarried in the big house, looking around nervously as if searching for something before their eyes rested with a gleam on my face. A friendly, even reverential smile broke out on their faces, something I had never experienced in my captive days. Then they walked backward toward the door, making a bow when they stepped over the threshold, giving me the embarrassing impression that this elaborate courtesy was intended for me.

XIII

U pon my second return from Shucun village to my company, my status underwent a radical change.

Carl personally instructed that I was to work with him in his office every day. I accompanied him to press briefing after press briefing, where I made PowerPoint presentations about the customs and people of Shucun village and their gratitude to our company. Carl had frequent media exposure as representative of HZ Communications China, becoming something of a spokesman for its corporate culture. Public regard for the company soared as it totally upstaged SME. The 800-million-dollar contract had been awarded to HZ by public opinion.

Of course, contract tenders are not democratic elections. The company's public image of an exemplary corporate citizen working for the public good was wind in the sails, to be sure, but success could be assured only when all possible wrinkles had been smoothed and all connections sewed up. Therefore my most crucial work was to be accomplished through my old specialty: attending dinner parties. The difference was I no longer attended William's parties but accompanied Carl to dinners hosted for government officials of all ranks and stripes.

In early autumn when Shanghai was at its most beautiful, I was a nightly regular patron at grand and elegant restaurants of this city. I got into Carl's Mercedes Benz in the mellow wine red light of sunset and got carried back to my apartment in a taxi under a sky filled with spinning stars.

I no longer remembered all the names of so many of those restaurants: Tanfu Cuisine, Fortune Fountain Seafood, Jing Shark's Fin Restaurant, Tiandi Restaurant, Jade on 36, Sir Elly's Rooftop Restaurant & Bar, and others. Their décors were characterized by gilt motifs, the ubiquitous crystal chandelier, full-length windows, quasi-antique or cultural landmark themes; then of course there were the rooftop views of the Peninsula Hotel or the Shangri-La, or the windows of Three on the Bund, Six on the Bund and Seven on the Bund, overlooking the Huangpu river and commanding a breathtaking view of the Oriental Pearl Tower. The Thai Village Shark Fin Restaurant inside the Grand Soluxe Hotel in the Hongqiao district was eliminated from the competition because it didn't meet such lofty standards.

What were some of the cornucopia of delicacies I had tasted? My ears, more than my gustatory and gastronomic organs, had retained the memory of a few, such as: stewed shark fin in brown sauce, leopard coral grouper with bamboo shoots in cream, gratinated Australian lobster, drunken crab in vermicelli soup, agate sea cucumber, braised *fo tiao qiang* (Buddha Jumps Over The Wall) with deer penis and Chinese caterpillar fungus, beef tendon and fish lips, foie gras with truffles, scrambled eggs with sea-urchin, prawns with lime, Asian abalone and choice lamb chops made by bona fide French chefs.

The sight of a table graced by carcasses of all shapes and stripes always mystified and bewildered me.

I was reminded of those animals kept by the Shucun villagers as their source of meats, the ugly short-legged black pigs and the mountain chickens with a protruding belly, called by locals "lazy chickens." Each household possessed a maximum of two or three "lazy chickens" and not every household had a black pig. These constituted for them an alternative source of meats other than game harvested in hunting expeditions. In the eyes of city people, this consumption pattern represented a progressive trend; only, the variety and quantity were too measly by far.

The villagers never kept their captive animals in enclosures; all they did was feed them. The pigs and chickens normally ranged freely on the plain; they sometimes stole unnoticed toward the foothills and were to all appearances going to disappear into the dense forest. But if one tried to turn them out, they would run back in a fluster to the trough, never to go far again.

Come to think of it, they had quite a carefree life, not having to worry about foraging for food and sheltered under a roof that shielded them from the cold night; and they lived a reasonably long life. Their keepers did not lightly kill them for food; only at major festivals or sacrificial rites did they select some aging animals to be slaughtered in a solemn ritual overseen by Shuren. The meat was not immediately consumed. After the villagers had just a taste of a small portion of it, the rest was smoked and preserved to last them for a year.

This life of scant meat and low-fat diet was trying on me. The plain and the forests teemed with a variety of animals—wild rabbits, fawns, blue sheep, yaks and countless others. They never shunned people; a few of them sometimes even ventured near the troughs during the twice-daily feedings of the villagers' pigs and chickens to sample the food out of curiosity, although they never lingered too long in the area. I had no doubt that if the Shucun villagers enclosed a few parcels of land on the edges of the plain and corralled these animals into separate quarters, they could easily build up a huge animal farm and turn Shucun village into a cornucopia of wild game that put a different variety of fresh meat every week on the table of the villagers.

I described this vision to Shuren.

It was only with great effort that Shuren finally understood what I was talking about, and for the first time he did not display that soft smile of approval on his face, as if he much preferred the half basket of wet firewood I used to gather to this smart suggestion I just brought up. With a shadow of a frown and scratching his heavily creased face, he seemed to be trying hard to find a way of putting it to me.

He said: "Those animals do not belong to us. They are our neighbors. Would you try enticing your neighbors into a big house, lock them up and feed them, force them to breed and then make the whole lot of them into smoked meat for your future consumption? If we arrogated to ourselves the right to domesticate them and make them into the meat on our table, then they could equally keep us in cages and fatten us to be made into their meat. Would you like that kind of life?"

I protested lamely: "But what about the pigs and chickens you keep?"

"I don't like that either," Shuren said. "But those pigs and chickens probably need to live like that. We provide them with a carefree life, in exchange of which they agree to become our meat in some future year. It's like a contract. But I still don't like it. I've always thought that if our ancestors had not lured them in by feeding them every day and thus taken away the incentive for them to go back to the forests to forage for food themselves, to experience an independent life, they would not have become so afraid to leave the feeding trough and these protective roofs. This contract may appear to have been agreed voluntarily by both sides, but in the final analysis it is a scheme on our part to ensnare them."

I fell silent, reduced to salivating vicariously at an imagined Brazilian barbecue. Then my thoughts went back to the cities, curious places where most denizens, like me, had to have meat for every meal to feel fulfilment. I could eat half a roasted suckling pig on offer at the Yue Zhen Xuan Cantonese Restaurant. Even at KFC I could obliterate at least five pairs of chicken wings for lunch. This would be impossible in Shucun village; it was unthinkable for them to kill five chickens for just one meal for one person.

Now that I thought about it, I was shocked by the cities' capacity for slaughter. I was a very ordinary employee of a foreign-capital enterprise; in every office building in the city there are at least a thousand people just like Kevin. Every city block has at least a dozen such buildings and there are thousands, maybe many more, of city blocks in Shanghai. A daily lunch consisting of five pairs of chicken wings 365 days a year is a most ordinary wish for an individual like me, and the city could easily feed all its residents a daily lunch like that. Every night on the perpetually lit stage of Shanghai, sumptuous banquets too numerous to count are consumed with gusto.

I dared not imagine how many of our animal neighbors we fattened and slaughtered to supply the city's gustatory needs.

In addition to me, Carl took to the dinners a large entourage including his assistants, his secretary, the personnel manager, the deputy manager of treasury, core members of the sales department and the bidding team, the composition varying slightly from dinner to dinner. Clearly they were all in Carl's immediate circle of trusted aides.

They flanked Carl at the table in a fan-shaped formation, evoking an image of the black pigs and "lazy chickens" clustered about their keeper in Shucun. On their best behavior before the food, they looked at Carl with an admiring, meek smile.

Among these people, I was the only plebeian, outranked by all the rest. They held important powers while I was not even a supervisor. But I was the person seated to the immediate right of Carl, at his request.

Half way through every banquet, Carl would put down the wine glass held in his right hand and pat the back of my left hand on the table and say in an oratory tone: "Let me introduce Kevin to you. He is my closest old pal! We were colleagues twelve years ago, two low-level employees at HZ headquarters, drinking together and talking about women on the beach." Carl laughed with joviality and gave the back of my hand a forceful tap before saying with a raised tone: "Now we are still drinking together …"

Carl's words obviously were not intended for me, or for his trusted aides flanking him. An expression of embarrassment came into the faces of these people, who were now involuntarily sizing me up. I could see the doubt, annoyance, jealousy and studied disdain in their eyes. But I sat too close to Carl, so that when they turned their faces toward me they faced Carl too; when they listened attentively to Carl, they always made a point of nodding and smiling. Now the two different sets of expressions were in confused battle.

Carl continued: "... We are still drinking together; the two of us are simply inseparable. So, given this special relationship, don't you think he should drink up three glasses for me?"

Carl's words were directed at the officials sitting on the other side. One such official, already uproariously drunk, was insisting on toasting Carl with a nearly empty glass. He was not the most important official, but apparently not one to be easily put off either. The trusted aides on our side of the table hastened to echo the sentiment: "Kevin is really our boss's best pal!" After saying something to that effect, one trusted aide looked aside at me, as if to show me the corner of his mouth curled in mockery.

When glass after glass of excessive alcohol took its volatile effect inside my body, I would feel, on the back of the left hand, a curious burning sensation. Sometimes when Carl slapped on the back of my hand, I would feel enormously honored and moved and ready to drink up all the alcohol of the world for him. At other times, my head would remind me that I was merely a domesticated animal that most served his purpose at the particular moment, that I should feel insulted.

Carl and I had not again mentioned the conflict at that infamous emergency meeting, as if both of us had suffered amnesia. On the few occasions when there were just the two of us, we would talk about any and all subjects in an atmosphere that was more cordial than ever.

Jessica often joined these dinner parties, now a very important person to all appearances, and she drank little.

Seated to one side, she would from time to time eye me through her wine glass with an expression that was almost but not quite a smile. When I met her eyes and tried to decipher her thoughts of the moment, she would lower her eyelashes with composure. If she sat next to me, she would still put right the chopsticks that had slipped off my chopstick rest and remind the wait staff to fill my wine glass or tea cup. But even as she did these things, she was all the while in convivial conversation with those sitting across the table without deigning a glance at me.

Since she vented her wrath on me on that occasion, we never had another private talk; no more coffee together, no more MSN chats, only work-related emails and texts. I had chalked it to a form of punishment she meted out to me; that was fine with me. But now it turned out I was more like a Chihuahua following behind her high-heel slippers, that she could pick up with three fingers and stroke affectionately when the fancy took her and the next moment throw back down without a word.

One night, in the latter half of a dinner party when all table mates were in an inebriated state of reduced consciousness, Carl went to the lavatory. On that particular evening Jessica and I were placed on either side of Carl. Jessica, across the vacated seat of Carl, her beautiful face slightly flushed with wine, said in slowed speech to me: "You see, isn't this great? Wouldn't it be better if you had done it much sooner?"

These words convinced me that she was not in the least drunk. As for me, it didn't matter whether I got drunk or not, I always felt fidgety, ill at ease and increasingly inept at connecting with humans.

The "radicals" of the company were on a roll and appeared to have gained the upper hand by an overwhelming edge. But strangely the "moderates" did not show the least nervousness or unease, or were in any rush to take counter measures, at least as far as I could see.

William still organized his dinner parties with the usual frequency and was the center of attention and adulation, deploying his comic talents to the thrilled screams of girls and women of the entire company. Old John still made his elegant appearance at company meetings, with his hair smartly styled and a different silk scarf tucked inside his shirt collar every day. At the end of the work day, he still drove his white BMW to a place of "pleasure" arranged by William.

An atmosphere of peace and prosperity reigned in the company. You'd think there was never any infighting and that I had worried in vain.

I accepted the invitation to one of William's dinner parties. In William's words, on the occasion of my second return from Shucun village, another "welcome back" dinner in my honor was in order. This was the third such dinner hosted by the marketing department in my honor. I still worked at the department after all and it was not every night that I was given the assignment of accompanying Carl to functions. So I came with William's party once again to the Xianghuqing Restaurant. I didn't want to know, nor was I capable of knowing what this particular dinner meant. I was simply going to drink myself under the table.

It turned out better than I had expected. They still toasted me one after another, but with restraint. Nobody forced me to drink. I imagined that was prearranged by William. The atmosphere, how should I say, could even be characterized as one of gentleness and amicability. I almost felt regret and contrition for having left the warm hearth of this group and at the same time some bewilderment. Had the office infighting that nearly sent me to my death been a figment of my imagination?

After several rounds of toasts, it came to William, who said with a falsetto voice and his two front teeth biting the rim of his glass: "I don't drink; I never take a drink ..." It set off an uncontrollable burst of merriment. William's imitation was dead-on, and everybody realized he was mimicking Mary. Pushing up his upper lip with a finger to bare his front teeth, he continued his act: "Drinking is bad for one's health. You shouldn't drink so much ..."

I had noticed that Mary was absent from this dinner party.

Maybe her son was sick or there was some other important reason for it.

William had barely finished that sentence when Edmond, the origin of that burst of merriment, emulated the parody by pulling up his upper lip and saying in a funny tone: "I really can't make it tonight. My Dongdong has no one else to take care of him ..."

William gave Peach, who sat next to him, a nudge. For a moment Peach hesitated, which I interpreted as a disinclination to join the game, but she was pausing only to think of a better way to do a more accurate portrayal. Pulling her full head of curled hair back, in the manner Mary usually pinned her long hair back, she bit her lower lip with bared upper teeth, which instantly transformed her face into a contorted mask. Surprisingly, despite the rigidity, she still managed to compose her features into various expressions and to talk.

My face must have become flushed. It was hard for me to remain seated at this table, where they got kicks out of insulting an innocent person, particularly when that person happened to be Mary, whom I had vowed to protect. Even though the humiliation of Mary took place behind her, out of her sight and earshot, it still embarrassed me no end, all the more so because I didn't even have the guts to confront them; instead I humored them by laughing with them and making a show of admiring their creativity.

The game continued, as one after another parodied Mary; the more debasing, cruel and grotesque the caricature, the louder the applause and cheering. William called out the names of those who did not volunteer to play the game. They started tepidly and perfunctorily parroting her, but amid the crescendo of cheers of those watching, they somehow got excited and couldn't stop their wry-faced apery.

I was reminded of that game of deer hunting, in which Aqingbu and Ah Rong gave chase and scored with ease, wasting not one of those 26 arrows and that one-year-old blood-covered fawn bristling with arrows, looking like a hedgehog, staring fixedly at the blue sky with those eyes frozen in death.

My mind slipped back to what Shuren said to me, that when one animal bit another to death it was always for a legitimate reason; humans, on the other hand, are different. Humans have always bitten or killed gratuitously, to satisfy some mysterious inner needs and for fun.

Boisterous laughter dinned in my ears; those pale distorted faces seemed no longer able to return to normal and fangs seemed to have sprung between their lips. I instinctively put a hand up to my mouth in a sudden panic, fearing on one hand I was also growing fangs and worried on the other hand I still had my normal, flat mouth, definitive proof that I was not a member of the human race. As I was being torn between the two conflicting emotions, William pointed a finger in my direction. Covering my mouth with a hand, I shot to my feet as if having been scalded and staggered toward the door. I heard Thomas say: "He is probably going to puke."

I stumbled along the corridor of the restaurant looking for the exit. Through the crack of the door of the reserved banquet room, I saw Thomas performing in my place, baring his front teeth with relish to the table. In my flight I kept bumping into the walls. I felt thick fur sprouting on my clumsy body, exposing me as the emotional monster that I was. I tried to hide my true face from those humans but the harder I tried to get out of their sight, the more futile my effort to find the door out of the restaurant.

Old pal, I'm now disclosing a top secret of the company to you.

The following day Thomas asked me to meet him in the refreshment room behind the copying machines. With a grim face he produced a pack of Parliament menthol cigarettes with one mg nicotine content and handed one to me. I waved it off, saying I never smoked. With a shadow on his brow he lit one for himself with an air that accentuated the incongruity of his child-like face. He said through the curling smoke: "Old pal, did you know that Old John is being transferred back to headquarters ahead of time?"

I asked Thomas: "Why did you tell me this?"

He looked gravely into my eyes as if wishing me to see the sincerity in his eyes. He said: "Nowadays it's hard for college graduates to find a job so I consider myself lucky to have landed this job. Can you put in a word for me? A minor figure like me doesn't get to pick his boss. If I have a choice, I'd rather follow you guys."

I never relayed what I heard from Thomas to anybody. I made this decision the first time he passed so-called inside dope to me. I had no wish to be a spy again and wasn't eager to build up credit with anybody. Besides, I once fooled Thomas by feeding him "information" and I couldn't be sure if it was his turn now to fool me.

I believed that by not telling anyone about it, I would avoid being tricked and tripped. But there was a general unease in the air at the office, where the two factions vied to get the upper hand. Everyone could clearly sense an imminent coup d'état. Most, like me, had no idea which way the balance would tip, whether one would become cannon fodder in the battle or rise to higher positions on the coattails of the victor. The female employees wondered if they should get pregnant at this juncture; the male workers didn't know if they should search the help wanted websites for a new job or consider taking out a car loan for a new automobile.

In every corner of the office people were trading in a whisper tone gossip of all shapes and colors, recounting conflicting versions of "intelligent analysis" or airing personal gripes. A dense pervasive anxiety hung in the air. I kept my lips sealed; I, a weak-willed corpulent man, was constantly warning myself to clamp shut my mouth. I possessed a possibly true piece of privileged inside information, but I could not tell it to or discuss it with anyone. I agonized over the truth or falsity of the information.

In a recurrent scene in my dreams I took the elevator up to the office of the vice president, knocked before letting myself in and said to Carl: "Old pal, I have an important piece of information to pass on to you ..." then I would wake up with a start. I must have contracted the disease of anxiety over keeping secrets, a prevalent new syndrome associated with office infighting much discussed on the Web. In the end that piece of information made a fool of me, whether it was told to others or not.

I took the elevator up to the office of the vice president, knocked and let myself in, having of course made an appointment with Carl's secretary ahead of time. Carl straightened up from his large desk and his genuine leather chair and smiled at me with a glowing face.

I said haltingly: "I was going to ask you if this camp ... I mean the side you, Jessica and the rest of us are on, if this camp has the confidence to drive out Old John and William."

Carl answered with a peal of hearty laughter: "That's a foregone conclusion. What's on your mind? Tell me."

I was encouraged by Carl's glowing face and buoyant mood.

So I said in stutters: "How should I put it ... since this side is assured of victory, there's someone who'd appreciate a small favor from your side ..."

"You want to know who? Well, it's Mary I'm talking about, that divorced woman raising a kid, with a very white complexion. You must have seen her. What did she ask me to convey to you? Oh, she didn't say anything to me. I took it upon myself to ask if it is possible to transfer her to another department, say, the sales or planning department, for either of which she is qualified because of the nature and ambit of her work experience. If she stays in the marketing department, William will continue to bully her whenever there's a chance. It is really hard on her. Carl, given that the demise of the old order is imminent and Old John is leaving, can't you deliver a few of the suffering masses from their misery? Would you help please?"

The air congealed for a few seconds before Carl answered

without changing that pleasant smile: "Ah ya! That would give us a bad name and it is against company rules."

It dawned on me that this battle had not been fought to bring salvation; that had never been on the minds of those who took up arms. By an accident of circumstances I now stood on the side of the winners and I had secretly congratulated myself for it. But now it seemed the coming glory was a dubious one. It had nothing to show for it but the casualty figures. Humans dedicate their days, their lives to doing such things to each other, with absolutely no benefit to either side.

In the descending elevator I suddenly realized how very stupid I was. Just as Jessica had berated me on numerous occasions, I was ludicrously naïve. When Carl never thought about transferring me out of the marketing department into the safety of his sphere of influence, despite the fact that I followed him around like a faithful dog, working my butt off, how could I believe that he would lift a hand to help Mary, who was absolutely of no interest to him?

The dinner parties in honor of government officials finally came to an end and I returned to my cubicle in the marketing department exhausted and desirous of a long vacation. William asked me teasingly if a fourth "welcome back" dinner party should be planned.

Then he called me into his office and handed me an order form with which I was to take possession of a set of broadband and computer equipment that had been approved for Shucun village as an addition to the satellite phone project. He said he had to trouble me to make another trip to Yunnan to deliver the equipment to the company's office in Kunming and while there I was to oversee its installation and see to it that those savages sitting between their sheaves of wheat and their fire pits would enjoy the same amenities as in any well-equipped internet bar and any home theater in the living rooms of any upscale apartment building in Shanghai.

XIV

News of the return, once again, of Deputy County Chief Liu's son from the city, spread in the County of Xuyang farther than the shot from an artisanal gun. I seemed to have grown to like the way Liu Yushang, oozing alcohol from every pore of his body, took my neck in a stranglehold with his arm and bragged to everyone willing to listen how much I took after him.

In light of my account of a kid injured by a bear last time I was in Shucun village, Liu Yushang prepared two artisanal guns and insisted on having two men with guns at the ready follow me around in Shucun for the duration of my stay, saying the measure was to prevent wild beasts harming his "eldest son." I strenuously objected to the precaution, saying: "It would look bad, as it would give me the air of a bandit chief."

I finally succeeded in persuading the armed guards to go back to town but they didn't give me the option of refusing the two artisanal guns.

Taking the trail paved with soft pine needles, I returned once more to Shucun village, amid a golden light shimmering like the reflection of the sun's rays off fish scale and a shower of falling leaves. This time around there was no Shuren waiting outside the big house for me. He was presiding over a funeral.

The 7-year-old Mila did not survive past autumn that year, the growth of his young body having stopped and a look of disbelief persisting in his still eyes. The three welted scars remained sprawled on his frail, exsanguinated shoulder. Finally he would no longer be startled awake by the cries of a flight of birds and he no longer needed to be bothered by his own qualms about using the long bow to kill.

On this day the wind blew crisply and the sky was high and clear, with not a wisp of cloud, as if welcoming a genie not meant for the human world back to his celestial haunt. Everything on this earth was subsumed in this beautiful azure; there was something in the air that could be sorrow, or post-sorrow relief. From the foothills rose Shuren's prayer: "*Hu-ma-hu-ma-la-ni-yeh, hu-ma-hu-ma-ge-la-jia* ..." I heard a surge of weeping, mixed with a low, animal-like whimper. From a hollow in the far hills a wisp of black smoke spiraled up, accompanied by an unplaceable odor; suddenly the whimper broke into a long heartrending, frightening wail that long echoed between the mountains.

I did not attend the funeral. I made a habit of eschewing such occasions because I wouldn't know what to say. Besides, it occurred to me that someone might not be so keen to have me see the sadness in his eyes at the funeral.

Aqingbu pounded my left shoulder with his huge right fist and then hammered my right shoulder with his left fist. Then he drew me to him and took me in a vigorous embrace. After we hugged, he insisted that I should go with him to his home to enjoy some fresh venison. His heartfelt joy at meeting me again, particularly at a moment like this, moved me in no small measure.

I was eager to set up the broadband and computer equipment as soon as possible. Although not as practical as a tractor, it was better than a phone. The villagers were not in the habit of phoning and there was nothing they needed to call the outside world about. A computer linked to the internet was a different matter. I certainly did not expect them to surf the web pages, send and receive emails, but it occurred to me that they could watch TV shows online and download movies. If I succeeded in teaching them how to do that, it would at least become a source of entertainment for the villagers.

I had no idea which big shot in the "upper management" decided to supplement the gift of the satellite phone with this extra item. I told myself: "At least this proves that those office politicians have not gone completely brain dead because they are still capable of bringing some practical benefit to the villagers even as they are using the project mainly to boost their own performance in the company."

I remembered having touted the virtues of the outside world to Aqingbu and that more than once he had expressed the wish to learn more about the outside world. Now I could finally make his dream come true. Through internet TV, he could see not only the stories, real and fictional, that took place in Shanghai, but also countless faces from the other side of the globe. I could see that his heart was still filled with deep sorrow and an air heavier than the forged iron used to make scythes hung in his house; it was possible that the novelty of television programs was just the thing to take his mind away from all that grief and help cheer him up.

I also planned to install Skype on the computer, so that even after I returned to Shanghai, I would still be able to have face-to-face chats with Shuren on the webcam-equipped computer in my apartment. Wouldn't that be wonderful!

After the equipment was set up and tested, I planned to spend several days training the villagers in groups.

Most villagers were fascinated by this 27-inch LCD monitor; they felt the smooth, shiny screen with their hands, astonished when they saw their hair pulled straight toward it because of the static. Some insisted that the thing was filled with the clearest water from the Jinsha River. Others said: "This is an egg shell that has not properly developed. You can see streaks on it." Still others wondered: "It must be a piece of the sky that has fallen to earth! When I lifted my head to look at the sky today, I found it smooth and shiny just like this thing, and clouds traveling across it."

I picked up on that idea: "Indeed, things move like the clouds on this screen." With a click of the mouse I opened the sina.com.cn home page, splashed with rows of pictures and text and Flash ads blinking on the margins. When I looked over my shoulder, I found that the villagers had all shrunk back ten paces, all looking at me in panic and confusion.

Aqingbu came forth in long strides and courageously touched the screen of moving images with his hand to show the others: "This is a TV. I told you before that those people laughing or crying in this box are real people who live in this world, farther away than those mountains and even at the other end of the world. You didn't believe me then."

The villagers asked: "People? Where are the people? All we see is lines and blocks just like those in our wheat fields."

I switched over to internet TV: Fifth Avenue of New York City was teeming with pedestrians and cars; on a giant glass wall attached to a tall building a commercial about Apple computers was playing, and a pretty blond woman dressed in black and high heels was shown choosing jewelry at a counter in Tiffany's.

Aqingbu cried sharply: "Look, look at those people!"

The villagers who had fled from the monitor surged back toward it and formed a tight cluster about it.

After watching with an approving smile the entire demonstration, Shuren told me that he had no need to see the outside world, that no matter how big that world might be, there were people everywhere, therefore it didn't make a difference where you were.

After the astonishment of the villagers over the LCD screen ebbed, it was my turn to be astonished by Ah Rong.

In this country of self-sufficiency in everything from food to clothing, where even the solar power generator was only just installed for this project, you didn't expect anybody to have the faintest idea how to operate something like a computer. They couldn't comprehend why the screen display would change when you moved the mouse, or what kind of relationship existed between that virtual reality and reality. But Ah Rong was an exception.

If he had grown up in Shanghai or any other big city, there was no doubt in my mind that he would have been a computer whiz, and would even have been recruited away by Bill Gates. He seemed born with an ability to recognize those little signs in the pull-down menus, and after a brief bashful moment was able to wield the mouse to transport himself all across the virtual world, like a driver who knew the roads like the back of his hand. He soon mastered all the software applications I taught and could even use them in ways I didn't cover. I suspected that if his Han Chinese were better, and if he had a little knowledge of English, he should be able to pick up the skills even faster. But even now, by rote learning, he could already reinstall the entire system all by himself. I had never expected anyone in the village to master this skill.

Later when I was back in Shanghai I had frequent video chats with Ah Rong in the afternoon; it was an exhilarating experience. Although Shucun village was much closer to Shanghai than to the United States, Ah Rong's face-to-face chats with me on the monitor had for me more of a wondrous sense of transcending time and space than my video conferences with American counterparts in the Silicon Valley.

It was also thanks to this gift of Ah Rong that I gleaned from his accounts the later events.

This was a particularly long autumn in Shucun village. After my departure, the temperature miraculously went back up for two weeks and the wind also became as soft as in late summer. Sitting at night in the new concrete building on the hill to watch internet TV and smelling the fragrance of the maturing crops in the fields became the favorite activity of most Shuncun villagers.

Among those villagers, it was always Aqingbu who was loath to leave and watched the programs the longest. Even though the people on the screen often froze in mid-action (for example, the player app would buffer three or four times for someone in the picture to climb one step of a staircase) due to the slow internet connection, Aqingbu never lost his patience but kept his eyes glued unblinking to the screen. Like a mesmerized kid, he crouched on the floor, biting his fingers, his huge bulk blocking half of the screen. A man who did not easily let his grief show, he sometimes stared vacantly at the screen, half of his broad face in the shadow, probably thinking if he could delay his departure some more, he would shorten the time he'd have to spend facing that empty little bed and his wife's unending tears before going to bed.

Ah Rong downloaded some movies. He said that Aqingbu liked some of them so much he had replayed them several times. He tried to describe those movies to me but I never really understood what movies they were. Judging from the subject matter, I'd guess they were probably movies adapted from Jack London novels.

For days on end Aqingbu sat in reverie in front of the LCD screen. When a note of clanking swords crept once again into the wind rising in the plain, Aqingbu all of a sudden pulled himself together and said to Ah Rong: "The television has shown us every corner of the world, people everywhere doing all kinds of great things. This is after all the humans' world. Why should we continue to behave so wretchedly, self-debasingly and ingratiatingly toward the bears?"

He said: "I realize only now that humans are really the masters of this world. They kill wild beasts and in the process turn themselves into heroes. Although I have never known these people, an inner voice has always said the same thing to me all these years. I think that must be because we think alike as humans."

As he uttered these words, a determined gleam appeared in Aqingbu's eyes and a dark red color of excitement rose in his broad face. He shot to his feet and headed straight to Shuren's big house, with the parting words: "I'll go talk to your father."

What Aqingbu never could wrap his head around was

something else. Mila, a tender-hearted kid who hesitated even to use his long bow against a wild rabbit, had never dreamed or believed that the bears, who enjoyed such human trust, could hurt him. This shock would accompany him to his grave or, put in another way, that swing of a mother bear's paw killed forever his trust and belief in anything to his dying days. When Aqingbu stroked him in his sound sleep, he would wake up with a shudder and would then look at his father apologetically, wide awake yet rigid in body. It was a heart-wrenching memory for Aqingbu.

Shuren said to Aqingbu: "Quit thinking like that. You know that the mother bear misjudged the situation. She was just trying to protect her cub. Animals don't bear ill will; they behave the way they behave solely out of an instinct for survival."

Shuren added: "Don't forget that one of the principles of being a hunter is never to have hatred in your heart."

Aqingbu said: "I'm doing this for all the parents of Shucun village who are worried for their children. If I kill that bear, our courage and power will conquer them, and no bear will ever dare again hurt our children."

Shuren sighed: "You just violated the prohibition against hatred; now you are rationalizing your intention out of vanity and an obsession to win."

Aqingbu said: "Who doesn't have these sentiments in his heart?"

With those words, he placed his huge hand over the left side of his chest, and with a slight bow, backed out of the house.

Assembling the best "hunters" and the strongest young men of the village Aqingbu told them that this expedition was not to hunt down deer or rabbits but a bear, the bear that killed his son!

He said: "This is a hunt in violation of village laws. There will be no Shuren praying over the killed game for their peaceful passage to the beyond. There will only be the courageous warm blood that has gone to sleep in our hearts all this time. We alone are the masters of this plain! Every corner of the world has been conquered by humans. It's time we conquer this plain of ours.

Even if the bears did generously offer a home to our ancestors, one thing will not change, and that is humans will overcome the bears. I will prove it to you! Those who are afraid can leave now."

Aqingbu's speech set the black heads of the assembled men billowing like flames. Some though put forward the idea that if Shuren was not coming with them, might it not be appropriate to ask the eldest son of the Deputy County Chief Liu to come back and for that corpulent man blessed by the gods to preside over the ritual of the hunt?

Aqingbu pointed at the concrete house in the distance that housed the computer equipment: "It is indeed he who's issued this sacred edict!"

Aqingbu and Ah Rong each carried one of the two artisanal guns I left behind. The rest of the expeditionary force were armed with broad swords, spears and iron sticks and carried on their back the most powerful long bows and full quivers of arrows. The large contingent set off on the trail of the human-faced mother bear and her cub. They did not smear their bodies with the special fragrance called *suma*, so that the bears would not think of them as hunters of game, but as people foraging for mushrooms in the forests, or logging timber to build fences.

That mother bear was not hard to spot. According to witnesses near the river, the white moon-shaped patch on her neck was outsized and could be seen even from the side. I imagined it to be something resembling the shirt collar of an office lady turned out to overlap the lapel of her suit. This feature enabled Aqingbu to quickly identify her. Two cub bears were playing near a tree. They must have eaten a lot more than they used to in preparation for hibernation, for they looked more bloated and awkward in movement than before.

At a signal from Aqingbu, the hunters spread out into a large circle that completely sealed off the escape routes of the three bears. Those wielding iron staffs and broad swords stood in the front row, and those who had their long bows drawn back and at the ready were placed right behind them. Ah Rong, on the other side, fired a shot into the sky, which startled the two cubs and caused them to break into a run straight toward Aqingbu. With his long bow drawn taut into a quivering full moon, Aqingbu let fly an arrow that hit a cub on its left shoulder; it missed its throat barely by an inch. As the cub tumbled and fell, the mother bear reared up as if crazed. It was unmistakably the mother bear they were looking for; under her neck was an extra-large moon-shaped white patch.

The hunters had been waiting for her to stand at full height! At a loud command from Aqingbu, countless arrows flew from all directions; four or five of them pierced its belly and shoulders. After a moment of stunned disbelief, she surveyed the surrounding scene with a look of incredulity. By this time Aqingbu had rushed up to the bear and brought the steel barrel of the artisanal gun forcefully down on the side of her head, the violence of the blow sending the stock of the gun flying off. With a crisp cracking sound, the mother bear swayed as blood spurted from below her furry round ear. She bent down to shield the two cubs and turned around in panicked flight, but iron sticks were waiting for them in the other direction. The iron sticks were hurled at them; when they dodged, more arrows rained down on them.

The mother bear went berserk and rushed at those trying to bar their flight, in an attempt to clear a path of escape for the cubs. She struggled with five or six strong men and soon threw two on the ground; more enraged men threw themselves at the bear. It was a fierce battle never seen before in the plain and the fury on both sides was now at a feverish pitch, like a dark cloud accompanying a rain storm and rumbling thunderclaps tumbling and rolling on the hill. Humans and the bear were bleeding, leaving trails of blood on the hill as they were locked in mortal combat. From afar the blood blanketing the hill looked like huge magic figures painted by the gods with a brush dipped in cinnabar.

The humans were in disarray and the encirclement fell away. That crazed, blood-covered mother bear did not run away after striking down a young fellow on the outermost line of defense, but reared itself up to glare at the humans with eyes red like blazing flames, glaring at us as only a woman full of sorrow and anger would, Ah Rong described the scene to me later.

He said to me from the other end of the video call: "Fat One, you know I have not really learned how to fire a gun and I was afraid to hold it horizontally for fear of misfiring and hurting someone. But in that moment, what could I have done? My quiver was empty and the mother bear was going to get away. So I mimicked those people on television, aimed and fired two shots at her. Her body jolted violently, probably hit by one of my shots. She tried to rush at me and I pulled the trigger again. Following a loud report, her eyes instantly went inert and her huge bulk staggered. I did not again fire, nor did I rush up to give her the coup de grace by plunging my knife in her.

"We all knew then that this mother bear now belonged to Aqingbu.

"A chorus went up: '*Xia-lu-wa, xia-lu-wa, xia-lu-wa!*' Aqingbu went forward amid the shouts. His arms were bleeding and his clothes torn, his copper-colored body, strong like a King Kong's, glistened with sweat and blood. His eyes were blood-shot and the muscles of his face quivered as he unsheathed from his waist an eighteen-inch straight-blade dagger, which he had honed the night before. When he walked toward the bear with his massive shoulders spread out, he looked scarcely less stout than the mother bear and he had sustained only minor injuries. None of us therefore doubted that he could easily dispatch the mother bear, and thus personally avenge Mila's death.

"It may sound in my telling that everything went slowly but in fact it all happened in an instant. He whipped out his dagger, blocked the mother bear's retreat, and there was a steely glint as he raised it. At that instant he paused for the briefest second. Nobody knew why he suddenly got distracted—say, by a softening of his heart, or perhaps by the dazzle of sunlight glinting off the steel blade? In the pause that lasted only for the duration of half a breath, the mother bear's paw already tore into his chest. With a muffled gasp, he flipped his wrist and plunged the dagger into the mother bear's throat, almost burying the hilt into the bleeding flesh.

"The bear and the man entangled in a fierce struggle rolled off the cliff, with the mother bear landing first, knocking a big hole into the ground and flattening two patches of plantings. We wrested Aqingbu from the bear and for good measure fired three or four shots more at the mother bear. The two cub bears in the meantime had escaped—the mother bear's breach of the blockade had created that opportunity for them.

"Aqingbu was clearly not going to make it—his chest was torn open and blood was spurting out of the gaping hole. Holding him in my arms and weeping, I asked him: 'Why did you hesitate just now? You could have killed it easily with your dagger. What came into you?'

"With his eyes open and his mouth agape, he seemed to wish to speak but only gasps issued from his mouth. Bringing my ears close to his mouth, I could hear only intermittent, gasped out words that sounded vaguely like: 'A human's face … was the face of a human …' With every few words that struggled out of his mouth, blood spewed out of his chest. Finally he breathed his last breath. When he expired, his eyes remained wide open, with a look akin to puzzlement.

"For a long time afterwards, from the time of Aqingbu's burial to his wife's remarriage, I was in a daze, as if I were living in a dream. I obsessed about that same question: Why didn't Aqingbu grabbed the opportunity to easily dispatch that mother bear with his dagger? Why did he hesitate? It was a mistake the number one "hunter" of Shucun village could never have made! And what did those dying words—the face of a human— mean?

"Whenever I was not busy doing something, I would without realizing it myself half close my fist and imagine the situation Aqingbu found himself in on that fateful day; I would pull out from my waist an imaginary 18-inch dagger and raise it at the mother bear's throat. What unusual thing happened at that moment? I imagined before my eyes the mother bear, bathed in blood and its fur disheveled, arching its back and rearing up with the greatest difficulty, bracing for a final fight with the enemy wielding a sharp blade.

"Then it dawned on me one day. When the mother bear reared up, poised for attack, its height was almost comparable to that of Aqingbu. When Aqingbu got ready to lunge at the bear with the dagger, he suddenly saw a face closely resembling a human one, a human face on a bear's body riddled with wounds; maybe his eyes met those of the mother bear, eyes of a female human filled with sorrow and despair. He was petrified by this sight at such close range. For a moment he was no longer sure if the slaughter was right or wrong. How could he still plunge a dagger into its throat when confronted with such a face?

"A human face."

Ah Rong came to the end of the story. His Han Chinese has improved a lot, I thought; clearly he benefited much from watching television shows online.

In the wake of the simultaneous deaths of the mother bear and Aqingbu, the Shucun villagers who went on that fateful hunt were in a tremulous state of excitement and agitation. Back to the village with spent shotguns and broken weapons they vied to tell the story of the gallant, bruising fight leading up to the mother bear's death. They each brought home-brewed corn wine to the concrete house on the hill and drank all night, although every hand holding the wine bowl still trembled. They became closer than ever before, clasping each other's shoulder, as if their complicity in the unwarranted slaughter had bound them together in some kind of shared honor and glory, and, for that matter, shared sin if any. They cried uncontrollably over the loss of Aqingbu and laughed exultantly over their so-called triumph. In weeping and laughter they tried to bury the lingering doubt deep in their heart. And finally they collapsed with a saturation of alcohol, a warm glow of excitement on their faces and contentment in their hearts.

The carcass of the mother bear was not brought back to the village, for its meat would be tasteless and its fur damaged and unusable. Those people slayed it for the sake of slaying it.

When the hunters woke up from the corn wine, they concluded: "The mother bear killed Aqingbu and destroyed our crops with its fallen body. It deserved to die!"

The Shucun villagers echoed the sentiment: "It deserved to die! It deserved to die!"

XV

I was already on my way back to Shanghai long before these events.

On the day I flew into Shanghai, still encumbered by a suitcase, I was hauled away to Cashbox Party World, a karaoke establishment in Fuxing Park. Outside in the park swept by a bone-chilling night wind under a sky offering scant light from the moon and stars, the dim lamps lining the park lanes stood half hidden by the plane trees with yellowing leaves. Inside the Cashbox, the lobby with a glass fountain was amply illuminated, bright as day and flashy neon signs vied for attention.

Both factions in HZ Communications China were present; a succession of white BMWs, Tonga Green Land Rovers and silver gray Mercedes pulled up at the entrance and were left in the care of the valets. In small groups, the men walked in chatting and bantering and the women arrived with linked arms. The three largest private rooms had been reserved, toward which we made our way behind the ushers. It was a puzzling turn of events, leaving me clueless about what had happened or what was lying ahead.

Company dinners and annual gatherings were par for the course, but karaoke was a rare format, reserved for the entertainment of clients, and even then, a KTV or night club with a better ambience and décor would have been preferred to a mass-consumption, self-entertaining place like the Cashbox, normally a favorite for graduation parties and the like.

I recalled a practice at the headquarters of HZ Asia-Pacific, whereby major personnel announcements were made at a karaoke party attended by staff, after everyone got drunk and exhausted themselves by belting out song after song. The format was used as a send-off party or a consolation prize; it was said to be part of a more humanized approach to human resources management.

The practice had its origin in the elimination of the entire department of personal communications. At the end of the karaoke party on that occasion, a whopping one sixth of the headquarters staff had their employment terminated. In another instance, in the wake of the eruption of a scandal involving HZ bribing local officials, the vice president in charge and two branch managers resigned over the affair, only three days after this vice president was acclaimed as the king of karaoke in the company.

This mean-spirited practice had ruined the appetite for karaoke for some, who would suffer toothaches, stomach cramps and intestinal spasms and dryness of mouth the minute they heard the intro to a song. I was one of these people. More, though, plunged into this deathly game smacking of axes with an enthusiasm incomprehensible to me, as if it didn't matter on whom the axe fell, even if it were to fall on themselves, as long as they got to enjoy a wild party before death. Or maybe they already knew they were not the intended victims and therefore were in a ghoulish mood to revel as they waited for the sacrificed ones to be served on the table dripping with blood. Even as now, in the slowly ascending glass elevator, the female staff were eagerly consulting each other on what delicacies they were going for at the buffet and the male employees bragged about how many cases of beer they each would consume that night.

As I stepped out of the elevator I saw Jessica standing in the corridor, dressed in a long, dark coffee colored knit skirt, with diamond studs on her ears and around her neck a fringed shawl with a pattern of alternating orange and dark red. I wasn't sure if she had gone home to change into this outfit or had worn it to the office that day having had prior knowledge of the evening's event. Supporting herself on one high heel, she was drawing circles on the carpet with the other, as if waiting for someone. When she saw me, a smile broke out on her face. She waved to me, a friendly gesture I had not received from her for a long time. It was such an unexpected honor that I did a double take before realizing she was signaling me to follow her into a private room.

The gathering had not started to pick the songs and on the screen was a boisterous group of young men dancing and singing. I had no idea who they were for I had long ago lost my appetite for pop songs. There was a din of laughter and banter in the large room; only a few narrow slots were left on the crowded banquettes and people were chatting in small groups or consulting the beverage menu. Prominently seated at the center was, surprisingly, Old John, who was busily gesticulating to the female employees seated at his right and left, obviously absorbed in some game involving toothpicks.

Jessica's reason for bringing me into that private room escaped me. Was she assigned to that room also? As these thoughts churned in my mind, she had already sat down in a slot she found not far from Old John and was beckoning me to sit next to her.

It is just a fun party. Don't give it too much thought, I told myself.

Carl was not in the room. I heard his booming voice on my way to this room and turned my head toward the source of the sound and found him standing in the next room.

Scanning the room I found William absent also. He must be in the room across the hall then, for I didn't see him in Carl's room. Thomas was seated in a location closest to the screen and had his hand poised officiously over the keyboard for song selection as he asked each one in the room what song they would like to sing. He had the air of wanting to double as the evening's wait staff. After a round of asking, he turned to Old John again, who said with a wave of his hand: "I'm no good at singing, really. Let the others begin."

Thomas showed the utmost reluctance to do so, apparently uninterested in encouraging anyone other than Old John to sing; his posing as wait staff was for the sole purpose of unobtrusively serving only Old John. Sensing that soon someone else was going to order a song, he thought for two seconds before making up his mind and selecting a song. It was the song *Looking Back a Second Time* by the pop singer Johnny. Thomas picked the song probably thinking it was such an easy song that even Old John would have no difficulty humming a few bars.

Amid the clamors of those in the room, the mike was thrust into Old John's hand. As the first line crept across the bottom of the screen, Old John did not find the right tone and kept silent. At the appearance of the second line, he raised the mike but soon put it down. He clearly was someone very keen on protecting his public image; he was not going to make a fool of himself unless he was absolutely certain he could do it. It was only when the song went into a loud climax that he softly hummed along with the music and showed us what a tin ear was. His tone was far afield from that of the accompanying music; the people in the room weren't sure if they should applaud or not. He had enough sense to hum just one line before thrusting the mike at a girl at his side: "Why don't you sing it? You sing it!"

Thomas had the most wretched expression on his face.

Then others ordered songs and the marathon started: there were songs by Zhou Yunpeng, SHE, J J Lin, Jolin Cai … Sad to say I was really out of step with the times and all I could do was counting the bottles of Carlsberg littering the table. I glanced at Old John and found him even more bewildered by the songs.

Jessica got to her feet and somehow insinuated herself next to Old John. How did she get so intimate with Old John in the few weeks I was away? I watched her talk excitedly to him for a good while, and finally Old John appeared to nod his consent, whereupon she raised her voice above the ambient noise and said to Thomas: "Please cut to *Oriental Pearl*." She wanted to sing it with Old John. It begged belief that she would go to the length of digging out an old song as uncool and propagandistic as this simply to stoop to the taste of Old John.

At the end of the song, those in the room again hesitated to applaud. The lukewarm clapping quickly died down, in the fear that it would be interpreted by Old John as a Bronx cheer. Only Jessica appeared not to have noticed anything, and after finishing the last line of the song she turned to face Old John with the mike still in her hand and smiled encouragingly at him, and gave a few symbolic pecks in her right palm with the fingers of her left hand.

Old John said: "Pardon my shabby performance! Pardon!" Then he sat down with unscathed poise and composure and motioned me to sit by him too. Did Old John have plans to co-opt me for good measure after having engineered Jessica's switch of loyalty to him? Taking three toothpicks from the table, he challenged me to form with them a number greater than 3 but less than 4. A moment later he placed two beer glasses upside down on the table separated by a palm's width and took out a hundred-yuan bill from his wallet. I was to guess how that bill could be laid flat on the two glasses without falling off. The girls to his left and right began to giggle and laugh. Obviously he had already had occasion to show off his sleight-of-hand to them.

I could see that Old John was having a good time. Jessica in an excess of enthusiasm was still trying to get Old John to sing a few more songs. Thomas, too, with his fingers hovering over the keyboard and his head turned toward us, waited eagerly for Old John to give the command so that he could immediately add the song in. Three or four other colleagues rose from their seats and came over with raised glasses or coquettish urgings: "We came to this karaoke joint expressly to hear the president sing."

Then my heart gave a lurch: why were so many keen to make Old John sing to his heart's content? My experience at HZ headquarters told me that those who were most pampered at the karaoke event often turned out to be the ones the company was bidding goodbye to. Was Old John really on the way out? And this karaoke party was a send-off party for him? Yes, if even Jessica was being so solicitous toward Old John, it could mean that she felt a kind of guilt toward him and was bidding him final farewell on behalf of the faction of Carl.

At this thought I involuntarily turned my head to take a closer look at Old John. His checkered suit was smart but a little old-fashioned, double-breasted and vented in the back. His white shirt was made of a smooth solid fabric, with a purple-colored silk kerchief inside the dashing collar. But the superb material of his garment brought into sharper relief the unsightly creases on his neck and chin. A rash of age spots became visible upon closer scrutiny. His hair, combed back with fixing hair gel, looked at a distance dense and thick but at close range turned out to be insubstantial and to have thinned so much the scalp showed.

After a life of yeoman's service to the company, he finally failed to escape the fate of being driven out and seeing the promised options and pension terms turn to naught and naturally he would never be entered into the industry who's who. The thought prompted me to say with sincerity to Old John: "Why don't you sing a couple more? What is it you wish to sing? I'll order them for you."

Old John said: "Ah ya! I can only sing after I've got suitably drunk. So I'll pass for now."

I said to myself: so like me!

Unable to persuade Old John, Jessica turned around to egg me on. I excused myself on similar grounds: I need to drink enough before I can hit the high notes.

Jessica said she wanted to sing *Bygone Love* with me. I said:

"That won't do." Even though we already broke up long ago, that song still gave bad vibes. She said: "Why don't we sing *Love in Hiroshima* then?" I said: "Why did you pick out only those with sad endings?" The real reason for my reluctance was that female singers had an advantage with these two songs while the registers were way too high for men. After my horrible rendering of the song, Jessica clapped a few times in encouragement.

Everyone got pretty drunk by then. A server came in to remind us that it was past midnight and a discount rate would kick in. He looked like a wooden puppet whose lips moved without uttering a sound. Across the hall in the other room, there was a sound of metal and glass crashing and breaking, followed by a thud of some heavy bulk falling on the floor. A girl, probably drunk, wept and sobbed in a soft voice. Someone came over to offer idle gossip: a girl who was unlucky in love, office romance you know.

Thomas commented dryly: "Who cries nowadays over disappointment in love? Who gives a damn about who?"

A moment later he said in a lower voice: "How can there be romance in the office? It's always cloak and daggers and people are wary of each other."

When I looked again, Thomas had left his seat. He had become sick and tired of this altruistic role and had taken the opportunity to cross to the other room to investigate the fracas.

Old John staggered to his feet and fumbled with the keyboard for ordering songs. Suddenly the minority pop singer Han Hong's *That Crying Sea* leapt onto the screen. In an alcoholic mist, I thought to myself: he must have pushed the wrong button. Then I saw him locate the mike on a coffee table and plant himself in front of the screen and begin to softly clear his throat. When the intro ended, everyone in the room looked up in soberness: was that the voice of Old John? His voice had now fully opened up and soared like a big bird into the sky. In singing this folk song not made for a male voice, he was like a radio previously filling the air with static finally tuned to the right frequency.

With crinkled eyes and excited like a child, he pressed different keys. Jessica went over to help him find songs. He then performed a *xin tian you* style folk song originating in Shaanxi province and the *Paradise* made popular by the minority folk singer Tengri. With one hand keeping the lapels of his suit together and the other holding the mike, he sang with his back held ramrod straight and when he hit the high notes he would lean back and slightly lift his heels reminding one of the mannerisms of the singer Fei Yuqing. The room resounded with applause as he bowed with dignity and returned with equanimity and a faint smile to his seat, where he couldn't refrain from tapping out a lively rhythm on the table.

I suddenly had an urge to sing too. I went over to the keyboard and pressed a series of keys unobtrusively. I selected *The Plateau of Qinghai and Tibet*. After I finished the song, my colleagues looked at me with fresh eyes as if I were a stranger to them. They said this was coming to look increasingly like a contest between me and Old John for the title of King of Karaoke. Yes, Old John and I happened to be good at singing this type of songs. Oddly it was not so much a question of higher or lower notes as the fact that this type of songs had vocal ranges that were just right for our voice, and for some mysterious reason enabled us to bring it up out of our chest. Thus I could sing *The Plateau of Qinghai and Tibet*, but was completely defeated by pop songs in similar high registers, such as *Tears of Mona Lisa* and songs by Jeff Chang.

I was curious to know how Old John came to try those songs. Maybe, like me, he too had for years been tormented by his execrable performance of most songs he tried until he stumbled across this type of songs after who knows how many years.

In the early years, I had concluded I was an abandoned child of karaoke. I tried to imitate all my favorite male pop singers. After countless failures, I consciously selected only songs that were easy and bland as drivel and I searched the lists of karaoke favorites for songs that could show me to better advantage. In the end I remained a noise maker with a constricted throat, drifting from one octave to another and getting lost in the accompaniment. It is fair to say that had it not been for my despair and confusion and destructive low self-esteem, I would not have been driven to try *The Plateau of Qinghai and Tibet*, a song written for sopranos, nor would I have found out that I could also command the attention of a karaoke audience for five minutes.

Putting down the mike, I returned to my seat next to Jessica and Old John, and exchanged a smile with the latter. Old John handed me a just opened bottle of Carlsberg and said, patting me on the back: "Young man, after this drink, go sing another one! The alcohol will make you sing even better!"

He was right. I sang another song made famous by Tengri, *Blue Home Country*. Then Jessica insisted on ordering *Road to the Sky* for me and I did such an orotund rendition of it I felt my voice was bursting the room asunder. Amid even more deafening applause than previously, I did not return to my seat but squeezed myself into a gap next to Mary.

Mary had been in this private room since the beginning of the party. She sat at the end of a sofa closest to the door and leaned into the armrest, and had her arms folded around her knees. She was wearing a tight-fitting dark suit and the light and shadow playing on her face prevented me from seeing clearly her facial expression. By remaining silent all this time she had succeeded in making the others forget her presence. And in all that time I had been weighing whether I should go sit by her side.

I said: "Why don't you sing too? What would you like to sing? I'll select it for you."

Fully expecting her to refuse on some pretext, I was surprised by the quickness of her answer: "All right! Is there any other song you want to sing? How about my singing one with you?"

I was speechless for an instant, not being able on the spur of the moment to think of a song for two voices. It was she who had for a long period given me a wide berth, so her sudden friendliness astonished me. She gave me a smile indicating I shouldn't feel obligated to do it, and crossed with a light tread to the keyboard for ordering songs and quickly selected one and returned with equal briskness to her seat.

The song she picked was Rene Liu's *Madly in Love*. I found some similarities between her and Rene Liu in style and mannerisms. Her voice was thin, but her musical sense was perfect and she was able to stay seamlessly in sync with the accompaniment. After she sang the first part, Old John suddenly took it upon himself to pick up the mike to begin singing the second part. When he finished his part, Old John said, with fluent gestures, across many people, across me, to Mary that he had a particular liking for the Taiwanese singer Bobby Chen and that once he ran into Bobby in a restaurant and had a long chat with him as a fan. He then complained that the repertoire in this joint didn't even include songs by the Taiwanese artist Summer Lei. He believed that Summer Lei's songs were more suited to Mary ...

I suddenly felt sick. I pushed the door open and went, in uncertain, unsteady steps, looking for the men's room. Different songs wafted out of the rooms adjoining the dazzlingly bright corridor and assailed my ears from right and left. For a long time I wasn't able to find my way back to my room, nor could I tell the usher the room number.

I saw Jessica standing once again in the corridor. She gripped my arm with her warm hand and led me back to our room.

Mary and Old John were singing an old song *Understand My Heart*. This old oldie was so shabbily interpreted by them that I felt no need to applaud.

I thought Jessica would give me a ride home, as the valet had brought around her pink VW Beetle, given the fact that she had taken good care of me all evening and I was exhausted and drunk and had a suitcase to lug home. But then I thought: I need to see Mary home. With Old John ready to pounce on her at every chance, I couldn't stop worrying for her. As I stood thus in a dazed state on the front steps, Jessica already pulled away in her Beetle without even a goodbye through a lowered window. Maybe she too was exhausted. Old John's BMW in the meantime pulled up in front of me and braked to a halt. I wouldn't have accepted a ride from him, but then I saw Mary already seated in the back; so I said "thanks" and opened the door to let myself in.

At four thirty in the morning Shanghai was shrouded in a surreal dimness; the streets were deserted as if the entire city had suddenly been emptied of its hyperactive denizens and the mechanically advancing hands of the clock had ensconced themselves to some back alley in the unseen side of the metropolis.

There were just the three of us in the world, sitting in a white BMW with its headlights on. I said to Old John in the driver seat: "Take Mary home first." He didn't answer, nor did he object. For him to take Mary home first, he had to go out of his way. After he dropped off Mary in front of her community, there were just the two of us left in the world. Old John motioned me to sit in the front passenger seat.

Soon the car arrived at my apartment building. He switched off the engine and said to me: "Young man, I am very sorry to inform you that you have been terminated by the company. Tomorrow, oh, today rather, you can take a good sleep before reporting to the personnel department to complete all the formalities."

So it turned out to be me they were gunning for? I had a moment of hilarity.

Old John looked over his shoulder at me and said: "I've always had a favorite impression of you, so I told them I would take upon myself to be the one to give you the send-off. You can say whatever is on your mind; there's just the two of us here after all."

I shook my head. I was too tired. I opened the door and let myself out. He helped me get my suitcase out of the trunk. As he reignited the engine, I retraced my steps and knocked on the window. He lowered the window and met my eyes. I said: "I had wanted to ask you a question …" He looked at me with a smile, waiting with patience for my question or request.

I asked: "What made you try singing that kind of songs the first time?"

By the time I lugged my suitcase into the bedroom, the sky had lightened. I covered myself with the comforter and began a long, deep slumber.

I forgot how many days I slept like that, not stirring, not eating, not bothering to consult my smartphone or my watch, not wishing to speak and endeavoring to forget that there were other humans in this world. The bottles of Cola were depleted, the battery of my smartphone went dead and breakfast cereals and bread loaves grew moldy. In my dreams I heard the din of human noises but when I woke up there was only a death-like silence, disturbed only by the endless, maddening tick-tock of the bedside clock.

I got out of bed in the dark, and, with the comforter still draped around me, turned on my computer. There were no emails, no messages for me on MSN.

I put my cell phone on a charger. There were no missed calls, no texts.

I thought to myself: it wouldn't hurt to hide myself forever in sleep. But I couldn't even accomplish that.

Pacing around the room a couple of times, I found out I didn't even have the courage to open the door and go out. A few lonely birds chirped outside the window and the sky gradually lightened. The awakening urban noise of cars and people made me gasp for air. I didn't know how to enter that world of humans. I remained a prisoner in an isolated village, a captive that didn't need a prison guard.

I discovered the virtues of the Web. I could order meals, beverages, rolls of toilet paper, shampoo and down comforters on it. I left cash under the door mat and the express delivery guys left food and household items at the door. For a long time I was so absorbed in Warcraft games I had no thought for my real life needs. After I got tired of the games, I watched a dozen American TV episodes. I crammed my eyes and ears and my head full. I got interested in online forums of all types, commenting on hot posts by using different sock puppets and getting into back-and-forth debates, as a way of killing time.

One day the thought occurred to me that if I were a monkey, a lizard or a bear, I could still live in this way without anybody finding out. The idea scared me. Suddenly I seemed to sink further in a nightmare, into an even darker cave. From that moment on, I began to feel a panic never before experienced by me.

I logged into my company email and my personal email once again to find 21 unread emails, all mass mailings selling stuff. I started to set my MSN presence as "available" 24 hours a day, but still received no request for a chat.

I stared at Jessica online and hoped she could tell me why I was terminated without warning, and on the day of my return from my business trip too. Jessica must have prior knowledge of my impending termination. That would explain her uncharacteristically solicitous attention to me that evening.

I wondered if by staring intently at those mug shots on MSN, I would elicit some reaction in their owners, say, causing them to feel irritation or their ears to burn. Maybe I could ask Carl, or William? Would they tell me the truth? Or perhaps I could devise a list of questions a la Agatha Christie and find out by putting their respective answers together who was lying and who was telling the truth. What if they totally ignored me?

I also observed Mary's online presence. Her icon showed either "away" or "busy." I wanted very much to know whether she was worse off than before. But I realized that I was no longer in a position to show my concern about her. Fishing for her sympathy would be more in order.

I was plunged into an unprecedented anxiety. I was losing sleep and my head was as clear and sober as the sun at noon. But the sun at noon casts no shadows, and I was invaded by a sense that I no longer existed.

I dusted off my long neglected blog and tried to post on it interesting articles I found on the web. I often checked my blog a dozen times an hour, but I was the only visitor on the blog. I turned my cell phone back on and got great consolation from each and every one of the commercial solicitations.

I started to engage the express delivery guys in conversation and would talk to them, as I checked the merchandise, about soccer, traffic, love, the job market etc. until they said with impatience: "Can you do it faster? I still have many deliveries to make!" I looked forward to every telemarketing call; I would think of a host of questions to ask them: such as the floor area ratio of the apartment building, transportation routes, whether it carried a rental lease, thus shamelessly getting the salesman's hopes up.

I was too lazy to shave but I often stood for long anxious periods in front of the mirror in my bathroom. I wanted to ascertain my existence, to confirm that the image reflected in the mirror was indeed me. That image was so unfamiliar to me, with its vacant eyes, untidy stubbles, and the shape of a dirty ball. I involuntarily put my hand up to my chubby face to be sure that I touched it and that it also felt me. By the sunlight filtering in through the window, I stared long at my palms, arms and fat legs.

When I finally confirmed that I did exist, curiously I felt that the world I had experienced was unreal, that Carl never existed, William never existed and Jessica was probably a figment of my imagination, and that I never met a pale, frail woman named Mary. They were merely strangers on an MSN list and in a random permutation on the Web, we had added each other to our friends' lists, nothing more. And I had pieced together fragments of my dreams during a brief dazed moment in front of the bathroom mirror and had believed in their reality. As for memories of Shucun village, it was even more of a grotesque daydream. Did I really brush shoulders with many live bears, and even greeted them with a smile?

For lack of better things to do, I keyed in the word "bear" online to search for images.

The first hits were countless toy bears: such as a life-size beige-colored Korean teddy bear, sitting back to back with a little girl in the sun. And there was also a tan-colored teddy bear with an appearance familiar to me since a child. I was told that before the age of five I couldn't fall asleep without holding it in my arms. I liked the pensive look in its eyes, its extra soft chest, which returned with interest the warmth you imparted to it.

These were followed by the real bears, looking much like those depicted in elementary school textbooks.

As I scrolled down the pages, a photo of a "bear with a human face" hit my eyes. The image that had gradually faded from my memory now stood right before my eyes in a golden field of rape in full blossom. It was as if a dream had suddenly drawn back the curtains over my eyes and stepped into reality. The caption under the photo said: "The black bear, also known as Tibetan black bear, Himalayan black bear, or moon bear. They measure from 1.2 to 1.8 meters nose to tail. They inhabit forested areas, particularly hill and mountainous region, often active at altitudes of 3,000 meters and above and sometimes descend to lower altitudes and plains. Himalayan black bears have a thick black coat with a prominent white to pale yellow crescent on their chest, hence the name moon bear. They normally walk on all fours but are also capable of standing up on their hind legs. They are expert tree climbers and swimmers. They are omnivorous creatures whose diet consists predominantly of vegetation, such as berries, young leaves, bamboo shoots and mosses, as well as honey and insects, frogs and fish. The black bears' fear of humans is far stronger than humans' fear of them and they generally avoid humans and will attack them only when threatened or to protect their cubs."

Before long I found photos of the Bull Bear. The God of the Bears was clearly captured on film by the photographer from the side as it slowly walked through the jungle. The caption said: "The brown bears, wildlife under second class protection in China, have large body bulk, and their main habitats consist of conifer forests in cold temperate zones and alpine meadows. They are mainly distributed in Heilongjiang, Gansu, Sichuan and Yunnan in China. They are active generally in daytime and have no fixed haunts. They live primarily solitary lives. They are the second largest of the bear family, with a bulky muscle mass located above the shoulders. They have a coat with mixed colors, such as gold and brown. An adult brown bear can weigh six hundred kilograms and larger bears can weigh up to 800 kilograms."

So what I experienced in Shucun village turned out to be true. I was once Kevin of HZ Communications China, sent on a hardship mission in a community aid project, and that was how I arrived in that beautiful plain where bears were worshipped as gods.

Then I remembered the broadband and computer equipment in Shucun village and the fact that I taught Ah Rong how to use Skype. As I launched Skype, a notification box with an ice blue background and a snowflakes pattern popped up with "Merry Christmas!" splashed across it as well as a history of eleven missed calls from Ah Rong in two months.

It was in the afternoon of Christmas Day, Ah Rong told me, that Aqingbu died, together with the mother bear in a life-or-death struggle. Then he spent an entire week to fill in all the details. His account made me relive that familiar fear, not a human's fear of wild beasts, but a wild beast's fear of humans, or more accurately, a human's fear and deep abhorrence of his own species.

Ah Rong said: "Fat One, I wish you had come online much sooner. If you had spoken to us from the other end of the internet, maybe you'd have blessed Aqingbu and prevented his death."

I didn't know what to answer. I recalled Jessica's frequent

taunts that I lacked "people skills." Now how could I be treated as a god when I was not even considered a decent man?

I was on video chat nearly every afternoon from New Year's Day to the Spring Festival.

With increasing frequency he asked me: "What do people in your city do every day? Is it really like what internet TV shows us?"

I answered: "More or less." How otherwise could I have described to him this world in which I felt so helpless? I recalled having teased him by urging him to find himself a girlfriend through online chats. I said: "With your handsome looks, you will easily garner a large following of admirers on the chats."

After the Spring Festival, that string of anxiety in my head finally snapped.

I pulled the plug on the computer, drew the curtains and returned to my deep sleep. This time my dejection was total; I felt I was in the pits and had lost the will to climb back up the abyss, not deigning even a glance at the rim of the abyss.

It was my intention not to get out of bed, not to speak, not to heed any outside sound, not to order take-out food and not to breathe. Then I would in short order be gone with the wind like dust, vanish in the depths of the comforter.

One after another the fingers were gone, then the two legs, the elbows, the shoulders; the body was dispersed like a fog by the wind to scatter in a tenebrous silence. The soul, still sober and crystal clear, floated about in search of light. A shaft of light came down from the skylight in the big house to fall on a soft, wrinkled face. I had a sudden sense of coming home. There was a moist warmth in my heart and I was on the brink of tears, but I no longer had eyes or a mouth.

I wanted to say: "Take me back! I much prefer to stay forever on this quiet plain, in this big house of yours."

I wasn't able to utter a sound but Shuren seemed to have heard the voice in my heart. He answered with a gentle smile: "My child, no matter how big the world is, there are people everywhere and therefore it doesn't make a difference where you are."

Uncomprehending, I was on the point of asking why that was when Shuren's weathered voice started chanting: "*Hu-ma-hu-ma-la-ni-yeh, hu-ma-hu-ma-ge-la-jia ...*" And I felt I was rising weightlessly in the air, higher and higher. I saw once again the azure sky of Shucun village, the mountains ringing it and the beautiful plain in the shape of five petals. I saw the golden pumpkins drying in the sun on rooftops, children playing at the foot of the sacrificial altar and people spreading out to work in the fields; and this went on day after day.

This was not the entirety of the plain, but only a corner of it small like an anthill. Hidden behind the deep grass, near the tree roots and under the level ground was a vast world with dark winding tunnels, an untold number of spacious, comfortable caves where the bears slept in their secret world, their numbers probably many times the number of humans living above in the sun. They would wait until the sun was low and humans quieted down before emerging from their caves groggy-eyed to quietly forage for food and move about, a timid and bashful smile forever on their faces.

I saw that these bears also lived in the same city as we did, in the concrete jungle, in the vast, unseen world behind tens of thousands of walls, in spaces people never suspected existed. They hid in the depths of caves conveniently connected by a network of streets and roads, these emotional, clunky, sensitive creatures with frayed nerves, spending the long nights heaving silent sighs and peering with wariness and bewilderment at the world at dawn, then, going back to sleep again, exhausted and disoriented.

The ringing of my cell phone woke me from my slumber. I didn't know its battery still had juice left in it. I reached down and fumbled on the floor and found the cell. It was Mary calling.

Her thin voice sounded like a young boy's.

She said: "Kevin, did you just wake up from a nap? Or do

you have a cold? Have you tired yourself too much on your new job? You sounded a little down."

She said: "You are fine? I'm glad. I called to tell you something. But maybe you already knew." Here she sounded a little timid and hesitant, but it appeared she had made up her mind before the call, for the moment passed and she resolutely went ahead with what she started to tell.

The "something" she wanted to tell me turned out to be the thing I had craved to understand during my long self-imprisonment: the reason for my termination by my company. It was because of the additional equipment I brought to Shucun village in addition to the satellite phone, i.e. the broadband and computer gear. While picayune in cash terms, this additional equipment happened not to have been included in the budget submitted by HZ Communications China to the parent company for approval. This was not only in violation of company rules and regulations, but also contrary to the practice at headquarters.

The penny dropped! So it was William! William who handed me the order slip and told me to get the equipment, and made sure that I personally went to Shucun village to oversee its installation. It turned out it was William who engineered the whole thing to get rid of me!

Mary demurred: "You overestimate your importance! If the purpose had been to get rid of you only, William wouldn't have gone to all that trouble."

She told me: "Indeed it was William who proposed that the additional equipment be attached to the satellite phone PR project. As head of the marketing department, he put this proposal to the highest authority in the company in charge of the project. And the highest authority overseeing the marketing department should have been Old John, but this PR project was conceived with that 800-million-yuan sales contract in mind, therefore it was not inappropriate for William to have sought approval from Carl. William said to Carl: the donation of the satellite phone has already had a huge impact on public opinion. Why don't we for good measure throw in broadband and computer equipment, which won't cost much but will be the icing on the cake and the press will have a field day reporting this extra generosity."

It was a time when Carl was besieged by media photographers by day and hosted endless banquets by night, and had received private assurance that the deal had been sewn up. In the euphoria of a triumph already in hand, he unthinkingly signed William's request with a flourish of his pen.

The extra expense normally would have required Old John's signature, but William and Old John worked in perfect coordination. When William went to Carl for his signature, only days were left before the technical team was scheduled to depart Shucun village, which meant I must leave immediately for the village with the additional equipment to avoid any delay in the completion of the project. But Old John had taken a number of days of sick leave and stayed home, saying merely that the work should go ahead and the requisite papers would be signed by him after he recovered from his illness, post facto.

An old Chinese saying puts it well: tall trees attract the wind. Carl's frequent exposure in the media on account of the satellite phone project attracted the attention of the parent company. In the third quarter HZ headquarters conducted a routine audit of HZ China and found a cost overrun in the marketing expenditure. The first thing that came to their attention was naturally the item of the donation of a satellite phone, which per se was within the budget, but the supplemental equipment glaringly fell outside of the budget. And the funds were spent already, with only the signature of the vice president but without that of the president.

I asked Mary: "The broadband and computer equipment valued at a few tens of thousands of yuan was peanuts compared to the 800 million yuan of the sales contract. I could understand if William tried to cause me grief with this trivial matter. I can't imagine him stupid enough to attempt toppling Carl with it."

Mary said: "In the view of the brass at headquarters, while a manager with strong performance and the ability to bump up company earnings was a sought-after asset, an asset that ignored the headquarters rules was less desirable than an incapable manager who adhered to management rules. And William accomplished what he set out to do. The success of Carl's faction in getting that 800-million-yuan contract notwithstanding, Old John and William were bound to have the upper hand over them."

Mary explained everything with such clarity and logic that for a moment I nearly fancied that it was Jessica speaking at the other end, although her thin voice was a far cry from Jessica's mellow speech. I thought to myself: Maybe Mary is not as frail or weak as I imagined. Maybe she has never needed my protection. The proof was in the fact that I depended on her to provide the answer to a question that more than anything eluded my comprehension. If as she said William had used the ploy to cause grief to Carl, then why was I the one terminated, since I didn't even have the rank to put my signature to any expense invoice?

After a pause at the other end, Mary said with some hesitation: "Er ... you didn't know?"

Didn't I know that HZ headquarter could certainly not afford to let go Carl over this matter, for they still relied on him to get the 800-million-yuan contract for the company; but in order to make their authority felt, punishment had to be meted out.

Didn't I know that the struggle between Old John and Carl always found a temporary balance after some kind of compromise or expedient measure? This had been so all those years. The weights used to achieve that balance were scapegoats in the rival camp. It was a way to weaken the other side and at the same time clean out the sand in one's own shoes.

Didn't I know that after their consultation, Carl and Jessica reached the conclusion that the sand was going to be me. It was they—one claiming me as an "old colleague" and an "old pal," the other a trusted female friend of mine in whom I had placed utmost trust all those years—who did it. No wonder Carl avoided facing me at the finale and little wonder that Jessica made the special gesture of sitting next to me and sang with me the doggone *Bygone Love*.

The fact was I had guessed it all. Only, I had run away from that knowledge. Wasn't that so?

Mary's tone was apologetic. She asked in a low voice: "Hey, you all right?"

I'm fine. I couldn't be better!

In the wake of that karaoke party there were some others who were terminated in the same fashion as I. They were from the technical department and the financial management department. This I learned also from Mary. I drew a deep breath, wanting to get something off my chest to her. "Thank you, Mary. Thank you for calling me, Mary. You have been in my thought all this time. How have you been?"

Mary said in an even tone: "I'm fine. You are welcome. Rest well and don't let it get to you. I got to go now. Bye."

In March I read the news on the Web. HZ Communications China was the winner in the tender and formally signed the contract with China Mobile to provide custom-ordered network communications equipment and services in six provinces, including Yunnan, Sichuan and Jiangxi, with a total value of 780 million yuan. The accompanying photos showed Old John seated on the rostrum representing HZ Communications. He was photogenic and urbane and straight-backed in every pose, putting his signature to the contract, exchanging copies of the contract, shaking hands, smiling, dressed in a dapper old-fashioned suit, with a square of kerchief in his shirt collar. The three photos with a panoramic view in the center all clearly showed Carl and Jessica sitting in the back row as part of Old John's retinue.

One week later I received an email addressed to Kevin in both my work mailbox and my personal mailbox. The same day, my cell rang loudly and a text followed. The personnel department of HZ Communications China informed me that I was invited to present myself and report for work as soon as possible at the company the following Tuesday, i.e. tomorrow, or on any work day.

The equipment in Shucun village broke down and the organization department of the Xuyang County Party Committee wrote once again to the company, requesting the earliest presence of comrade Liu Kai to carry out an inspection and repair. It was agreed by both HZ China and HZ headquarters that even though the 780-million-yuan contract was awarded to them already, this PR project in Yunnan still needed to be properly attended to. Who but I—Kevin, who got the sack a long while back—had the requisite familiarity with the people and customs of that locality?

The personnel department went to the bottom of the pile of papers to find my staff registration form, with the number 89, filled out by me the autumn before last year. A young man waiting, like me, to get through the formalities, appeared to be fresh out of college, a lank fellow with a crew cut and a slipper-shaped face, quick to smile and with the number 233 on his staff registration form. With staff turnover and the expansion of business areas, HZ must have hired quite a few new people. I was hired as a new employee, an entry-level employee in the marketing department, with a three-month probationary period.

William didn't seem to recognize me, his eyes sweeping past me, as if I was transparent. No longer did he tease me about girls or romance, nor did he snidely suggest a "welcome back" party in my honor. It occurred to me then that I was now too insignificant to qualify as a target of his taunts.

Thomas on the other hand had some frank, private talks with me both as my supervisor and as an "old pal." He sat in the refreshment room holding his cup of black coffee and I busied myself with adding milk and sugar to my cup. He said to me: "I'll give you a piece of advice as an old colleague. My advice is: don't make futile attempts to be rehabilitated. Go find a job at some other company. What good will it do you even if you make that arduous trip to Yunnan and accomplish your mission with flying colors? You'll still be on probation when you come back and you'll be of no more use to them. They can refuse to renew the contract, with no explanation. Do you believe me?"

I did believe him. But I was even more aware of the frustration in Thomas caused by my rehiring. The maintenance of the Shucun village project fell squarely in his purview and I heard that he had volunteered several times to go himself to Shucun but with those in the technical team sent to Shucun terminated at the same time I was sacked, who would know how to get there and how to deal with those savages? In the end Old John preferred rehiring me to trusting it to his faithful dog.

Thomas rehashed his advice repeatedly. Hearing his double entendre and seeing the awkward rigidity his small, almost puerile, narrow eyes failed to hide, I was filled with secret amusement while thanking him with feigned sincerity and letting my indecision show, which nearly drove him crazy.

I knew they would terminate me at the first chance they got after I resolved the issues in Shucun village. I also knew that the technical team to accompany me would certainly include some trusted followers in Old John's camp. They would establish contact with Shucun village through my intermediary so that they would no longer depend on my good will. But I didn't care. I had such a strong urge to go back to Shucun village. If someone offered to pay my travel expenses, I'd gladly take that offer. It could turn out that I would pre-empt the company's termination of my contract by deciding to stay on in Shucun village of my own accord.

I was not fit for the humans' world. Maybe it was written in my fate that I should belong to that plain. Maybe I was indeed the eldest son of Liu Yushan, or a "bear with a human face" who had strayed into this city and had hidden all these years in bustling downtown Shanghai without realizing my true identity.

It was time to leave for Shucun. I had no wish to see Carl and Jessica. Luckily our offices were not on the same floor and they had no wish to see me either. But I did wish to see Mary before I left. Since my rehiring, she had not shown up at her usual desk, and was said to be on field duty.

What would I say to her when I saw her? I wished to say: you are the only person I still feel attached to in this world. Of course I would not have the courage to actually say it in those words. Maybe I only needed to look into her eyes, hold them and flash a cheerful grin. She would certainly avert her eyes in a demure manner, turning away, showing on her cheek a beautiful rosy spot against her fair complexion. She would know what I felt in my heart, I was sure. Then what? Maybe I could persuade her to come with me to Shucun village, taking her Dongdong with her so that the three of us could live happily and quietly in that paradise on earth, never to part again.

That morning I saw her on the way to work. At a street corner by the Hong Kong Grand Century Place Mall she emerged from a white BMW and bent down to say something with a smile through the car window before the BMW turned into the parking garage. She saw me. I was rooted to the spot not far from where she was, still in stunned disbelief, and the thought of looking affectionately into her eyes couldn't be further from me.

With an unaffected, polite smile at me and a ripple of her loose-fitting menthol-colored wool sweater in the breeze, she turned and entered the building. I felt I didn't get a good look at her expression; there was a pendant of some sort on her neck I had not seen before that dazzled my eyes in the sun. Her white ankles were laced in silk straps attached to her high heels, the latest wrinkle in that spring season; her pretty calves quickly disappeared in the shadows of the building. She had a spring in her step.

No wonder she knew all that inside dope. Should I believe rather that she was in that BMW for the purpose of collecting information in my behalf? She now had a new relaxed, cheerful look as if she felt totally in her element. Maybe she too had aspired to succeed, to go places, say, get transferred to headquarters, get into the fast track of career advancement in the Global 500 and to see her name in the who's who of the electronic communications industry, only she had not had the opportunity. I wondered if a black incantation was also embedded in that new pendant attached to her necklace.

XVI

I was finally able to leave Shanghai for good, freed from all attachments and cares and to return to Shucun village.

I asked Liu Yushan if I did not come to his office with a reference letter from my company and I had no association at all with the PR project, would he still be willing to drink wine with me in the future.

Liu Yushan gave two smacks on my head with his thick palm. He said: "That shows how heartless you are! Don't you think that Mazda of mine totaled by you cost much more than that darned satellite phone of yours?"

Although he overestimated by far the cost of the satellite phone, I knew he spoke from the heart.

This time the escort assigned to his "eldest son" was even bigger, because of the snow in the mountains that had not thoroughly melted, and also because of the incident of Aqingbu's death by a bear's paw the previous autumn. Ah Rong, at the head of a group of young men, waited for us at the entrance to the plain. Liu Yushan assigned four men carrying artisanal guns to me. The large contingent climbed hills and mountains, talking and singing; after nearly a full day's march in the crisp air, the Shucun in my dreams was finally in sight.

The satellite phone, the broadband and computer equipment were working like a charm; they worked even better than what I had in my Shanghai apartment.

The original plan was for me to find out which component had malfunctioned and the tech team would then be called in from the Kunming office with the corresponding tools and instruments. It appeared now that they could fly straight back home from Kunming.

I asked Ah Rong: "What's this all about?"

Ah Rong answered with a shrug: "I'd been chatting with you online when suddenly I could no longer get through to you. Since I wasn't able to put a call through to you, it could only mean the computer had broken down."

Then he laughed mischievously and gave me a huge hug with his strong arms.

I nearly burst out laughing too, but I succeeded in keeping a straight face and followed his words with the announcement: "The problems with the equipment turn out to be rather serious. I need a few days to thoroughly check it out. Comrades assigned to me by the county government will please go back to town for now. No need to take any messages back. I know how to get in touch with those colleagues of mine."

After the others were sent home, there remained just Ah Rong and I in the concrete house on the hill. Ah Rong suddenly told me with a grave mien that he had devised the whole scheme to get me to come back here because my help was needed in a more important matter. It was not something that concerned only him but the Shucun villagers as a whole, the future of Shucun village and the late Aqingbu.

He took me by the arm and led me from the house. Outside, the vast plain was shrouded in twilight and the night air was bone-chilling; the specks of unmelted snow in the mountains and valleys far and near glistened silver under the star-studded sky.

He told me that in his estimation this would be the best time of the year to hunt bears. Most bears had not yet waken from hibernation but the snow on the mountain trails had for the most part melted to afford hunters a way into bear country.

The grand battle had been well thought out in all its details and was to take place in a few days' time. This time they insisted on my personally reviewing the troops before they went into the sacred battle. I would be taking over the function that used to be performed by Shuren in a hunt.

No, no, no! I agitated my hands in a fluster.

With a hearty laugh, Ah Rong put his arm round my shoulder and led me back into the house. He warmed a bowl of wine and passed it to me with both hands. The way he acted left me with the feeling that I was a kid he was trying to sweet-talk. He asked me: "Do you still remember what Aqingbu said? He said that despite our martial skills we were inferior to you. You are our hero. You've introduced to us the guns, the phone and the computer. You've shown us that humans can make themselves more powerful than merely being able to shoot deer and gray rabbits, that men are entirely capable of conquering the clan of bears and conquering this plain!"

With the excitement of this speech, a flush rose in his cheeks and his muscular chest heaved, and there came into his eyes a look of unshakable resolve. He now looked more than ever like Aqingbu.

There were a total of seventy to eight people, maybe more.

Not only the certified "hunters," but all young and middle-aged men strong of body and agile of movement of the village joined the hunt. Some came carrying sharpened wooden stakes and machetes, others had daggers at their waist and bows in their hands, still others carried dried straw and iron pots. The large contingent spread out on the plain, bristling like a forest. Six men who brought up the rear each held an artisanal gun, with six others ready to take over from them. Obviously they had had target practice.

It was clear that Ah Rong had worked long and hard in preparation for this epic battle. He was attentive to details, displayed stamina and commanded his troops prudently.

Clouds scudded across the gray sky and a cold wind raged.

The sound of leaves and boughs thrashing against tree trunks gave the illusion of tens of thousands of wild beasts far and near roaring in the jungle. The snow on the trails had indeed melted; the wet, dark slush reflected the light filtered through the branches. Occasionally small particles flew in the air, hitting and stinging their faces; these were remnant frost on fallen leaves whipped up by the wind.

The troops spread out to flank a large area on a foothill, the battleground chosen by Ah Rong. The machetes glinted silently and the wooden stakes sharp as knives were securely driven into the mud. The battle line was close to a few hundred meters long. The lengths of the stakes above the ground stood uniformly at knee height, and the sharpened ends pointed up the hill at a 45-degree angle.

There was a deafening bang, which shook the leaves and caused the snow to crumble at places in flakes larger than raindrops. It was a shot fired by Ah Rong into the air. Barely had the sound of the gunshot died down than the ground started to shake under their feet and a rumbling noise rolled in from all directions. The "bears with a human face" had been wakened up. Here and there, in places never thought to harbor a cave, furry ears slowly popped out, like young bamboo shoots sprouting out of the ground near tree roots after a rain, followed by a head, then two front paws, half a plump body and a clunky rump. One after another, they came out, still in a daze after being aroused from their sweet dreams, walking unsteadily and pricking up their ears in amazement, a bashful, silly smile on their face, and clueless about what had just happened.

Men deployed to higher ground immediately started banging on tree trunks and the iron pots to drive the bears to lower ground, while the hunters lying in ambush at the foot of the hill had drawn back their bows to the limit, their arms trembling uncontrollably with excitement and tautened muscles.

About twenty bears were flushed from their caves and were fleeing, at ever greater speed, the din behind them. With their extra-sensitive hearing, the banging sounded to their ears like deafening thunderclaps; not being able to see clearly what was happening due to their weak eyesight only increased their panic and they instinctively tried to run as far away from the source of the sound as possible.

They were on the point of running off the hill and breaching the encirclement of the archers.

As they came within twenty meters of the hunters, the stampeding bears ground to a sudden halt. The bears themselves would not have had the ability to stop in the middle of a mad dash like that. It was the doing of the row of wooden stakes planted in the ground, which the bears with their poor eyesight could not see. The sharp stakes met the legs of the bears in frontal impact. Given the speed of their stampede, the momentum of a downhill run and their heft, it was easy to imagine how violent that impact must have been. Those furry, plump fellows fell one by one and writhed and wailed in the mud, or had their knees impaled by the sharp stakes.

A cub bear in the rear of the stampede could clearly hear the unusual noise ahead of it and the wailing of the wounded fellow bears. At once terrified and eager to come to their help, it ran faster. Suddenly it felt as if a sharp piece of rock pierced the thighbone of its left hind leg; it could even hear the fracturing of the thighbone. In excruciating pain, it reared up its puny body at the unseen assault, waving its still unhardened front paws.

At that moment the arrows flew like swarms of locusts and gunshots rang out. It felt a burning in its right shoulder as if something exploded inside it and its right front paw instantly went limb. It felt the ground trembling as if an untold number of heavy bales fell from a height into mud. It realized with terror that those bales could well be its fellow bears dropping down onto the ground one after another. In its blurred vision a row of shadows approached from a distance, their arms and faces smeared with a red pigment made by mixing ocher powder with pig fat, and the animal tusks dangling on their braided hair clinking. What kind of monsters were those? Its eyes bloodshot, angry, grieving and terrorized, it wanted to rush toward them in a last ditch fight with them, but realized only then that it was no longer able to move the wounded left hind leg, which trailed limply along the ground. In that instant the group of monsters with red claws was upon it.

It heard the lead monster say to the others: "How many times have I told you that it's easiest to take aim at a bear, for they all have this crescent on their chest. There, do you see clearly now? If you fire into the center of that crescent, it will have no life left to pounce on you."

The cub bear saw the lead monster raise an iron tube thing upon his shoulder only to change his mind and lay it down. Instead he took the long bow from his shoulder and armed it with an arrow. Before it had time to react, the ice cold arrowhead was already buried into its chest, with the arrow shaft and the tail feathers sticking outside. Amid a victorious clamor, its consciousness faded and blurred and the ground heaved up and crashed onto its back. At that moment it saw with clarity the monster's face that came within inches of its own—a face just like its own. In astonishment it felt algor mortis set in inch by inch.

Long bows, guns and machetes far and near were raised and billowed like waves in the ocean. In the foothills reverberated that familiar shout: "*Xia-lu-wa, xia-lu-wa, xia-lu-wa!*"

Long after the crowd dispersed, I saw a small, frail figure detach itself from the rain and stand all alone on that slope of mixed mud and blood. Shuren was wearing a loose gown with embroidered hems; water was dripping from his gilt hat ringed by six upstanding panels. He walked to the corpse of a cub bear, knelt down and touched its forehead with his hand as he chanted gravely: "*Hu-ma-hu-ma-la-ni-yeh, hu-ma-hu-ma-ge-la-jia ...*"

I walked over to him and crouched at his side. I held his soft, wrinkled hand. With one hand holding my ice cold palm, he kept the other hand on the forehead of the bear cub.

That cub sustained one gunshot wound in its right shoulder

and an arrow was buried smack in the middle of its chest. The aim had been precise and the penetration was deep. But Shuren's hand was stroking its left shoulder, as rain dripped from the tip of his nose and slipped along his grief-stricken face down to his chin. An old wound was clearly visible in its left shoulder beneath the hair, made by an arrow and healed into a scar. This was the cub previously wounded by Aqingbu, the child of that mother bear. It had in the end not been able to escape death at the hand of humans.

Shuren had come for the express purpose of sending those slaughtered bears on to a better place. He chanted incantations with his hand laid on the forehead of one after another dead bear, spending over two hours on the hill. I remained at his side; that was the only thing I could do.

All through the night I sat on my haunches in a corner of Shuren's big house, feeling confused and bewildered. I was no longer sure if I was a Galileo or a Satan to Shucun village. Nor did I know if as a human I should take the side of the bears or the side of my fellow humans.

Just before dawn I asked Shuren: what should I do?

Shuren's eyes continued to show charity and understanding and no reproach.

He said: "My son, the water in the Jinsha River always flows east, not due to the power of any one drop of water. Every drop of water has its own mission in life; it cannot will itself to stop. Do whatever you want to do; don't think too much or too long about it."

What I wanted to do was to tell Ah Rong that leaving those dead bears in the wild to rot away was not as profitable as selling the bear livers and paws harvested from them for cash that could buy the village a tractor or something of use. As a friend, it was only right that I should impart that common sense to him, although that common sense could also conceivably come from Satan himself.

Ah Rong said: "Fat One, I really have to hand it to you. You know everything! I have so many other questions I have been bursting to ask you. Why don't you stay permanently and be our village chief? Aqingbu would be pleased if you did. The villagers have been urging me these days to persuade you to stay. Or ..." He saw from the expression on my face that he was putting me on the spot, so he changed tack. He said: "Or are you willing to succeed my father as the Elder of the village? You know that my father has always had a special place in his heart for you. And we really need you badly."

On the morning of my departure from Shucun village, I said to that beautiful plain: "Thank you and goodbye!"

Ah Rong asked me why I must leave. I answered him with Shuren's words: "No matter how big the world is, there are people everywhere, therefore it doesn't make a difference where you are."

Ah Rong did not know those were his father's words. He thought I was giving him some kind of pep talk and answered with enthusiasm: "Fat One, you are right! I will soon turn this plain into a place just like the outside world. Just wait and see. I will not disappoint you!"

XVII

I arrived in Shanghai on an early morning flight and there was a fortuitous flight the very afternoon that I could catch to attend the annual convention of the HZ parent company and all its subsidiaries.

The convention had been pushed back until this time of the year due to delays in wrapping up the year's final accounts. After the annual conventions had been held at various venues in Southeast Asia, this year's host was Yalong Bay in Sanya again. I was very glad that I still had an opportunity to enjoy an all-expenses paid vacation before they sacked me. The lank young man sitting next to me was also very pleased. He was that new staff member with a crew cut and a slipper-shaped face and the number 233 on his staff registration form, fresh out of graduate school with a master's degree. I had just found out his name was Tony. "Wow! This company is really generous, paying every staff member, even a probie like me, to attend the annual convention at a seaside resort!" he said. "And I heard that this goes on every year. How lucky we are!"

I liked the way Tony always had a grin on his face. We were probably the only two passengers on that plane who felt content. And I was not sure whether the following year Tony would still be able to travel with the same contentment to the annual convention. Maybe he would no longer be in the mood to admire the sea of clouds outside the porthole, but instead would worry about how to get in the good graces of bosses, climb up the corporate ladder, and do his damnedest to get transferred to the parent company or prematurely agonize over the likelihood of being inducted into the who's who of the industry.

The convention was hosted at the Ritz-Carlton on Yalong Bay, a garden villa-style resort whose grounds cover several square kilometers, boasting a large spa at 3,000 square meters and a 2,000 square meter conference center, palm trees swaying in the breeze and roses in bloom everywhere. My favorite was the main building in the style of a palace combining Japanese and Southeast Asian architectural features and flavors. From the spacious balconies of rooms from the second floor up, guests commanded a direct view of the blue sea. The ground floor rooms had direct access from their patios to the outdoor swimming pools. My favorite activity was a barefoot stroll at dusk on the beaches of the resort or staring at the breaking waves lying on a lounge chair surrounded by sheer curtains dancing in the breeze. Tony and I were assigned to the same ground floor room with a garden view, probably because we were both on probation. It was actually not bad at all. I had expected to be put in the same room with Thomas, in which case I would have been forced to watch his contrived play-acting. Well, I had apparently overrated myself. Thomas was a supervisor and I was way down on the totem pole, so naturally my room would be outclassed by his by far. As for Carl, Jessica, William, and Old John, I certainly would never dream of waking up the following day to find with great embarrassment that I had anyone of their rank as neighbor.

We had clear skies and the air was dry and comfortable and we had no shortage of sunlight. I enjoyed wearing a T-shirt and shorts to the buffet breakfast alone. Tony, the young man that he was, liked to sleep in till late. I would sit on the long porch outside the restaurant, drinking milk and watching the shadows of the palm trees playing on the garden bridge and finishing my

Caesar salad and two fried eggs.

In meetings, the air-conditioned room was just the right place where I could catch a nap and tune out all the verbiage.

At lunch time, I eschewed the noisy lobby with its many big round tables where all the others had their mid-day meal. Instead, I would normally walk along the beach to the Mangrove Tree Resort, where the Thai restaurant there served the most genuine Thai food in Yalong Bay. Only, the portion was a little too big for a lone eater like me.

Dinners amply spiced up with alcoholic drinks were par for the course, so I skipped them. I would take a dip in the sea and just vegetate on the beach, draped in my bath robe, until the moon rose. If I felt hungry, I called room service before 10 PM.

Those were a carefree, pleasant few days. Occasionally I'd wonder what I should do for a living after I got terminated once back to Shanghai from the convention. But scenes of the rat race, the conflicts and scheming of the human world that rushed into my mind quickly tired me. So I put off wondering till later and seized the day to enjoy the fabled sunshine in Sanya.

In the morning before the day of departure for home, it was HZ Communications China's turn to present its report. Due to the huge number of its staff and the presence of the brass of the parent company, the meeting venue selected was a huge banquet hall with no columns to block the view. The hotel management made meticulous arrangements for the setting up of the rostrum, the lectern of the presenter, and several seating areas, each of which was provided with sound equipment and mikes.

I had come prepared to catch my usual nap, but this time I couldn't. I found out I actually longed to observe those old timers.

Mary didn't come. I ascertained that fact after unobtrusively surveying the scene three times. From idle chats I learned that she had to stay in Shanghai to oversee the furnishing and finishing of an apartment she had recently bought. She must be doing very well.

Both Carl and Old John sat on the rostrum, in intimate, private talk with their heads leaning together.

William sat in the first row of the seating area reserved for the marketing department, with his back held ramrod straight. I wondered what could be the reason for his high spirits. Thomas, seated in the second row near the door, was giving earnest instructions to an attendant about brewing tea and adding water. He fetched William's cup to the attendant to be filled with boiling water and took it back to William.

Jessica looked unusually pretty today, dressed in a coral red pant suit, her shoulder-length hair arranged behind her ear on one side. She was standing at the lectern, her eyes lowered, calmly organizing the PowerPoint presentation on her lilac-colored 13-inch Sony laptop. An attendant was helping her set up the projector and the projection screen.

The thrust of Jessica's report was the recent big 780-million-yuan contract finally won for the company with the joint efforts of the sales department and the bidding team. She spoke articulately and always with a pretty smile, lifting her eyes every so often from her computer screen and scanning those seated on the rostrum and the audience in all the seating areas, gesturing from time to time with her arms to illustrate her eloquent points.

Her oratory skills had improved by leaps and bounds. Only, she looked today subtly different from her usual self. I wondered if I was being oversensitive.

The PowerPoint presentation on the projection screen appeared a little washed out, perhaps by the brightness of the lighting in the banquet hall. At the mid-point of her presentation, the attendant dimmed the ceiling lighting. Half of her was illuminated by the projector and her beautiful face was lit by the reflected luminance. She was emphasizing the important implications of the successful bid, not only for the company's sales and profit but the company's chance to become, on the strength of this success, the largest manufacturer of communications equipment in the China region.

It suddenly occurred to me that I'd heard these words before. Those were Carl's mantra and it was somehow not right that it fell to her to utter them on this occasion. Implications for sales and profits, those are matters talked about by company brass. Who was she to opine about them?

As I mulled these thoughts over, I heard a low buzz of voices ripple across the room. Jessica shot up from where she sat at the lectern in the middle of her presentation. Now she was like an actor, standing in the limelight cast by the projector. Hundreds of pairs of eyes in the dark, cavernous hall were riveted on her unusual movement.

"Today I would like to make some personal comments at this convention of the entire corporation, in the presence of the vice chairman of the board of the parent company, Joseph, CEO Jeremy, and Deputy CEO Nelson. Why did HZ and not SME get the contract this time? Was our strength superior to theirs? Or did we have technical expertise they did not possess? Or was our bid documentation thicker than theirs? Admittedly our bidding team and all those in the company supporting our work worked very hard for it, but that was not the key to our success."

The whispering in the dark subsided, giving way to a stunned silence. At this point, Jessica reached down and pressed the Enter key. It turned out the PowerPoint presentation was not over yet and she had prepared a slide for her personal observations. Three huge English words appeared on the projection screen: Enterprise, creativity, and regeneration.

She adjusted the mike. "This is the key to our success and this is also the key to the future growth of HZ! The gentlemen from our parent company heard about the entire process leading up to the successful bid for the contract, including the donation of equipment to impoverished areas in Yunnan with a view to winning the trust and support of the government with the public perception of our company as one committed to public good. But it was an uphill struggle to do that work because it met with great opposition, opposition coming from inside the company. Hindrance of this nature exists in many other areas of the company's daily work."

She paused, and moved her eyes in the direction of the darkened rostrum, as if to steer the audience's eyes toward that hindrance. "I am talking about a member of the high management of the corporation!" Those words triggered another ripple of whispers and movements in the hall.

"If a member of the high management like that stays one day more in the company, then our efforts will encounter resistance for one more day. And if that person stays one more year then during that year the company will not know rapid growth. When the company doesn't have a future, I, as manager of the sales department, will have no future in the company. Therefore in the illustrious presence of the gentlemen from headquarters, I'd like to state here for their benefit that if that high management person still works at HZ Communications after the conclusion of this convention, then I will tender my resignation the first day I report back to work!"

There was another stir and buzz in the room. Some cursed and a few applauded timidly before stopping altogether. Nobody knew which way the incident would lead. Anything could happen at any moment. On the rostrum, the three chief executives were huddling but no one had yet responded to Jessica's challenge.

With a light cough, Jessica resumed with a calm tone. "What I expressed was not just my own opinion," she said with confidence. "I believe that ninety percent of the staff hold the same view but have not had the courage to speak out as I did. To prove that point I did a survey in my sales department." She pressed a key. Tables and a three-colored pie chart appeared on the screen.

How confident are you in the growth prospect of HZ Communications China? Ninety percent checked "Not sure."

What's the most important reason for your lack of confidence? A hundred percent checked "Conservative forces in power."

If the status quo is maintained, how will you plan your

career? A hundred percent checked "Seek employment with another company."

Snickers were heard across the room. I was suddenly seized by an ominous premonition.

Still standing with poise in the light, Jessica smiled. "Gentlemen from headquarters, if you are interested, after the convention concludes, you can ask the staff in this room whether they will stay with HZ Communications if there is no reshuffle in our high."

"Fine, if you find it awkward to ask such a question on an occasion like this, I will ask the question for you." Jessica turned to face the seating area reserved for the sales department. "Those who will hand in their resignation tomorrow please stand up."

An unprecedented hush was the response.

Anyone turning a size A4 page would have his wrist freeze in the act of turning the page, for the rustle of paper would be too conspicuous under the circumstance for the page turner not to be fearful lest attention would be drawn to himself. Those who had a moment ago been in an excited state and looking about now would allow the eyes of those on the rostrum to see only the top of their heads.

Biting her lips, Jessica looked like a lone actor in the spotlight who had read her line but was prevented from exiting the stage.

Carl kept silent on the rostrum, with eyes closed and a hand supporting a cheek, as if taking a nap and as if the whole thing had nothing to do with him. Old John too seemed unconcerned. He lifted the lid off his cup and was absorbed in carefully blowing away the tea leaf fragments that still floated on the surface of the hot tea.

A tsunami of indignation and sadness swelled in my heart. It was so unfair to Jessica, I thought. I wanted so much to stand up in response to Jessica's question, but I knew that doing so would only further embarrass Jessica.

My guess was that the whole thing had been scripted beforehand, with Carl being the scriptwriter and the entire staff of sales having promised to cooperate and threaten collective resignations. When the crunch came, everyone changed his mind, with Jessica alone in the belief that every preparative step was in place, giving her little speech and openly inciting staff to declare the intention to tender resignations. That was no way to treat a lady! Or maybe it was from the word go a setup job to get rid of Jessica?

Humans are really a hard lot to understand. Friend or foe? Well, human friendship is fraught with unexpected and unforeseeable twists and reversals. It is at a time like this that I feel most strongly I'm incapable of living among fellow humans.

There was the sound of a chair somewhere bumping against a table behind it, followed by a hush, then the light sound of another chair. The lighting attendant, possibly thinking the presentation was over, turned the lights back on, thus catching a male staff member in the act of embarrassedly standing outside in the corridor, close to the seating area of the sales department and a female staff member who had just got up from her chair and whose face showed an equally embarrassed look.

Obviously that female staff member, at the first sound of a chair moving, thought it was time for collective action and had rushed to her feet, while that male staff member could have stood up for the simple reason of answering an urgent call of nature, but then again he could have, in his inability to predict accurately how the situation would evolve, had stood up anyway and assumed a posture of needing to rush to the restroom, which he could easily modify to suit the turn of events.

But their worries were unwarranted. A few minutes later all the staff seated in their area rose to their feet. I only found out later that all sales people had some kind of weakness the manager knew of and could use as leverage, such as fraudulent reports of goal fulfilment in connivance with distributors, bribery, unexplainable discounts. Or maybe Jessica had promised high rewards for cooperation, but that could not be proved.

The expression on the faces of the gentlemen from headquarters changed. This time their huddle was brief. Deputy CEO Nelson got hold of a mike. "We will consider the issue raised by you." While saying this he made a hand gesture to Jessica at the lectern and pointed at the demonstrators in the sales seating area. CEO Jeremy called Carl into an adjoining room. Vice Chairman of the Board Joseph made a hasty exit through a side door.

Jessica pressed the Enter key to go into the next slide of the PowerPoint presentation. The big screen showed the English words "That's all, thank you!" which appeared pale with the room lights back on. She turned her head around to look at the slide on the big screen and smiled with satisfaction. The conference hall started to empty.

After the convention, Jessica did not resign. The sales department did not cease to exist. Old John was transferred back to HZ headquarters and reportedly installed in a sinecure in logistics. William and Thomas quickly sought other employment, of course not at the parent company but with two small companies in the industry.

Mary also left. She never answered my phone calls. A few months later she was seen working in the planning department at HZ headquarters. At least Old John had the ability to arrange the post for Mary. He did not let her down. That's more than I could say for myself.

Carl became the indisputable successor to President of HZ Communications China at forty-four, with a promising future.

Two months later at the expiry of my probationary period, I received a letter of appointment from personnel, to deputy manager of the marketing department. The position of manager was left vacant and I was the de facto head overseeing the operations of the marketing department. It was normal practice that, absent any outsider parachuted into that position I would become manager in six months and enter middle management at HZ Communications.

The letter of appointment had barely arrived in my inbox with an audible alert when Jessica called. Her voice was cheerful and friendly. "You still haven't invited me to dinner to celebrate your promotion. Are you free for lunch? Let's go to Zen Restaurant."

The same girl in a white skirt was playing the piano in the atrium, her long, slender fingers continuously stroking the keys to produce an endless stream of music just as the wait staff carrying trays of food formed another steady stream. Jessica wore a lime summer dress, with the platinum Guanyin pendant shining under her neck. She was as beautiful as ever and when she looked at me her smile was as solicitous as in old days. "What you did not understand before, you need to try to understand now, and what you would not do before, you have to get used to doing," she said in that even, steady Shanghai voice. "You are a great guy. You just need some more practice in honing your EQ."

On the same day Carl received me in the office of the CEO.

He stepped out from behind his huge desk in his usual unassuming manner and addressed me as "old pal," "old colleague," and patted me on the shoulder. He encouraged me to work doubly hard. After all it was he who groomed me for my present position, the least I could do was not to let him down in the watchful eyes of the staff. We then chatted about a wide range of topics, such as government officials found to keep mistresses, *cheng guan* (urban law enforcement officers) beating people to death during enforcement actions, the skyrocketing home prices, everything except the latest event over which we both seemed to have suffered amnesia. Then he asked his secretary to see me out.

In the wake of the Yalong Bay incident, not long after my promotion, three successive staff members in sales handed in their resignations and went to work for the rival SME, either as a result of another internal purge or unkept promises of rewards.

In autumn, Jessica was as expected appointed to Deputy

President of HZ Communications China. I called to congratulate her but did not invite her to dinner.

Six months later, Thomas reapplied for an opening at HZ and my department hired him. He reverted to calling me "boss," and adopted a deferential attitude toward me. After a period of observation, I found him to be a decent young man who was courteous and good at taking care of his superiors, had a sense of propriety and got his priorities right, was a skillful collector of inside dope of all kinds in the company, and an enthusiastic social drinker. Therefore I promoted him to be my assistant.

XVIII

I never went back to Shucun village again. After the snow blizzard of the winter of the following year, the tech department could no longer detect any signal coming out of Shucun village, and attributed it to damage done to the wires by the weight of the snow. But the company did not receive any communication about the matter and it had been quite a while since Ah Rong last emailed me. They were probably so busy with selling bear paws and bear gallbladders that they had long put me out of their mind.

The fact was I too gave little thought to Shucun village nowadays, except on those rare mornings, very early, about four or five, when I would inexplicably wake up earlier than usual, at an hour when shafts of pale early sunlight peeked through the cracks in the window curtains and when the city was yet to awaken with its work-a-day sounds, save for a few isolated bird calls, I would then have a sense that I was back in that big house of Shuren's, my normally agitated mind suddenly soothed by a vast serenity.

In those brief moments I couldn't help but wonder whether Shuren was still alive and well and whether the fire pit in his house was being kept filled by someone. And I'd wonder if the farmers, weavers, and hunters of the 272 households in Shucun village had retained the dedication to their work, whether they still remembered human dignity and courtesy in battle, and whether, at least in their minds, they still were willing to give thanks for the sky, the sun, the river, and the gifts from their neighbors.

I realized that to become and remain masters of the world and of all things was a demanding and fatiguing full-time job and they presumably would have little time left to bother their heads about such trivial matters.

In much the same way I woke up every day with the shrill ringing of the alarm clock, left my apartment in suit and tie carrying a briefcase, staggered back to my apartment half inebriated from a late night dinner party, and flopped onto my bed and fell into a heavy sleep, thus mixing into the human crowd 365 days a year, busying myself with fictional performance goals, profit without products, divination of the intention of my superiors, analyzing situations, establishing temporary alliances, eliminating the opposition, scheming all the time, and walking on thin ice every day. As expected I was promoted to manager of the marketing department, an unprecedented triumph in my life. For fourteen years I was marginalized, and peaked out as a shabby old supervisor. But in the fifteenth year I shot into the position of department head from a lowly probie.

Jessica always had a sweet smile for me; she said I finally "wised up." Carl highly valued my work. Of course this didn't mean I would continue in their loyalty simply because Jessica smiled at me and Carl thought highly of me.

SME had been trying to acquire my service through a head hunter, offering a luring position at high pay. I looked into their middle and high management echelons and found much fewer obstacles there than at HZ on my way up the corporate ladder. Therefore I just might take them up on their offer.

I was quite comfortable in the humans' world, really. Standing before the mirror in the restroom of the Huangpu Club at Three on the Bund, I looked at that corpulent being with a flushed face and a hollow look in his eyes, dressed in a coffee-colored casual suit by Ralph Lauren, his two hands just washed and not yet dried, and a watch from a new line of Piaget on his left wrist. I could now certify him as a bona fide human. Five minutes before, he was flattered, buttered up from left and right. But five minutes later, as I stared at myself in the mirror, I wanted very much to hurl this monster, body and soul, through the window into the Huangpu River so that I would never clap eyes on him again.

"Hey, Kevin, come out now! Everybody is waiting for you to start the next round of drinks."

"Are you all right? Are you drunk?"

I'm not drunk. I'm perfectly fine. The chauffer drove me back to my apartment in my Mercedes Benz. "You don't need to take me into my apartment compound. I wish to take a walk in the streets," I said.

What season was it? Spring, autumn, or early summer? I lit a 555, walked a distance, and sat down on the bench in front of a McDonald's. It was already 2:30 in the morning. A chilly breeze swirled through the deserted street, five minutes, ten minutes, as if humans had disappeared without a trace from this city.

The sound of wheels grinding on the pavement came from afar. A swarthy middle-aged man was pedaling a three-wheeled pedicab carrying a full load of big bears. Their height was comparable to the humans' and they had round ears, rotund bodies, brown fur, and a beige snout. In order to prevent their legs from trailing on the ground, a two and half meter high wooden structure was specially made and mounted on the vehicle. The bears perched on that scaffold, with the moon above their shoulders. They sat compactly together, with their legs dangling in the air, remaining silent in this wondrous night, pensive and with a bashful and lonely smile on their faces.

With a strong push of the driver's legs on the pedals, they slowly moved away out of my sight.

Stories by Contemporary Writers from Shanghai

The Little Restaurant
Wang Anyi

The Most Beautiful Face in the World
Xue Shu

A Pair of Jade Frogs
Ye Xin

Between Confidantes
Chen Danyan

Forty Roses
Sun Yong

She She
Zou Zou

Goodby, Xu Hu!
Zhao Changtian

There Is No If
Su De

Vicissitudes of Life
Wang Xiaoying

Calling Back the Spirit of the Dead
Peng Ruigao

The Elephant
Chen Cun

White Michelia
Pan Xiangli

Folk Song
Li Xiao

Platinum Passport
Zhu Xiaolin

The Messenger's Letter
Sun Ganlu

Game Point
Xiao Bai

Ah, Blue Bird
Lu Xing'er

Memory and Oblivion
Wang Zhousheng

His One and Only
Wang Xiaoyu

Labyrinth of the Past
Zhang Yiwei

When a Baby Is Born
Cheng Naishan

No Sail on the Western Sea
Ma Yuan

Dissipation
Tang Ying

Gone with the River Mist
Yao Emei

Paradise on Earth
Zhu Lin

The Confession of a Bear
Sun Wei

Beautiful Days
Teng Xiaolan